OLD
HABITS

Books in the Mackenzie Prentice Mysteries Series

October Fire
Buried in Treasure
Painted Lady
On the Edge
Old Habits
My Cousin Krissy (2026)

OLD HABITS

A MACKENZIE PRENTICE MYSTERY

MARY PIERCE

Seven Windows LLC

Book design and editing by Michelle Rayburn (missionandmedia.com)

Belfry bell graphic by OpenClipart-Vectors from Pixabay royalty-free images.

Cover art by Mary Pierce

First edition 2025

Believe nothing you hear, and
only one half that you see.

—Edgar Allan Poe

Villainy wears many masks, none so
dangerous as the mask of virtue.

—Ichabod Crane in *The Legend of Sleepy Hollow*

To the sisters of Ladycliff College,
Highland Falls, New York, 1971

Sister M. James Joseph,
Sister Mary Daniel, Sister Lawrence Marie

If you can hear from heaven, thank you for the example
you showed me of commitment to a cause, the patience,
kindness, and especially the acceptance you offered to me,
even though I came from "the other side of the fence."

Oh, and also for introducing me to Irish coffee.

CHAPTER ONE

T HAT SATURDAY MORNING, IN her room on the second floor of the Holy Assumption convent, Sister Mary Agnes made her small bed, smoothing the crisp white sheets and green-and-white-flowered quilted coverlet into place. She hummed as she dusted her bookshelf and the small wooden table next to her bed.

She dressed, as always, in her gray skirt and white blouse, topping the blouse with a gray cardigan and rolling the cuffs twice to hide the frayed sleeve edges. She tucked her gray hair under the white headband of her veil, letting the gray veil fabric fall to her shoulders.

After checking the full-length mirror inside the closet door, she nodded to herself, satisfied that she and the room were tidy enough to meet the day.

She picked up the empty teacup and its saucer from the bedside table. The delicate china cup was one of six held in high regard by the sisters. The story was that General MacArthur had visited Mother Superior's home convent in New York after

World War II. The idea that he drank from these very cups imbued them with an aura of mystique and celebrity. Were they worth anything? Probably only sentimental value, although they were Haviland china.

Mary Agnes always had a cup of Sleepy Time Extra at bedtime. The valerian helped her sleep, and at seventy-seven, she needed that help. Aches in her hands, her neck, and her back caused restlessness. Osteoarthritis in both knees had slowed her considerably in the last few years. And her right hip liked to offer a pop every so often. Sister Bernadette, younger than she, had recently recovered nicely from a hip replacement. Mary Agnes considered having one herself.

Teacup and saucer in hand, she turned off the bedside lamp and opened her door. The envelope was there on the hall floor, just like the others. Her hands shook as her heart thudded. She nearly dropped the cup. Looking left and right to ensure she was alone in the hallway, Mary Agnes picked up the note and brought it inside. She sat on the edge of the bed, trembling.

The index card inside was folded in half, just like the other two. Ransom note style, letters cut from magazines and glued to the index card. A single word: SILENCE.

A shudder ran through her before she folded the card quickly and shoved it back in the envelope. She walked to the picture of Jesus on the wall, took the frame down, and flipped it over. Loosening one edge of the cardboard backing, she pushed this envelope behind the cardboard with the others and secured the back. She hung the picture on the wall, straightening it on its nail. She touched the Savior's face lightly with her fingertips, closed her eyes, and whispered a prayer for her own safety.

And another prayer for the poor soul who was leaving the notes.

She gathered herself and headed downstairs for breakfast. The rest of the day progressed as expected, with the sisters rotating through their Saturday chores after morning meditation. Cleaning and polishing the floors, stairs, and railings in the convent, as well as the floors, pews, and windowsills in the church.

This week it was Sister Mary Agnes's turn to clean the communal bathroom on the second floor of the convent. She cleaned, scrubbed, and polished with a vengeance, distracting her mind from the notes. The three sinks, three toilets, three shower stalls, the claw-foot bathtub, and the tile floor sparkled when she finished, leaving the air redolent of Pine Sol and Windex.

After an early supper on Saturday—Mrs. Jensen's vegetable soup made from fresh garden produce, along with warm, homemade sourdough with lots of butter—Sister Mary Agnes walked outside to the church. Her final duty of the day was to check the doors on the church building, to be sure all was secure.

The early evening air carried a refreshing chill after the warmth of the convent dining room. She entered the church through the front door, genuflected, and took a seat at the end of the back pew. She loved moments like these, in the dim light of the wall sconces and the silence, imagining the voices of all the saints and sinners over the decades, rising in praise to the Lord, or quietly acknowledging ignoble deeds in the sanctity of the confessional.

Entering stained, exiting purified.

But there was no absolution for her, she knew. Not after what she'd done. The secret she'd carried for decades. Yet she felt the need to confess and was willing to bear the consequences, whatever they might be.

She heard a noise to her left, rose from the pew, and crossed to the bell tower door. Poor folks from the street sometimes slept in the tower. She couldn't blame them. These late October nights were cold.

As Sister Mary Agnes tugged the heavy bell tower door open, she thought she heard a voice. "Who's there?" she called into the tower.

She thought a voice whispered her name. Had she heard right? She stepped inside, and the heavy door thudded closed behind her.

The wind carried the voice again. Calling her name, no question.

"Who's there?" She assumed it was someone in distress. A poor, sick child of God needing help. "I'm coming," she called as she started up the curving concrete steps. "I'm coming." She rushed upward, as fast as she was able, her aching knees complaining, her hip creaking step after step. Near the top, she stopped and bent over to catch her breath.

From above, the voice, suddenly harsh, said, "Silence!"

Just like the notes. Someone knew her secret shame. Sister Mary Agnes raised her hands, pleading with the shadows. "No, no, you don't understand. I have to tell. What I did was wrong. I just did as I was told, but it was wrong." She started to cry. "Please, God, forgive me."

The voice, angrier now, shouted terrible things about hell and damnation. Sister Mary Agnes could take no more. She covered her ears and closed her eyes, crying, "No, no, no!" She fell backward, the base of her skull hitting the edge of a concrete step below.

The pain was immediate and intense. She cried out as her body continued tumbling downward.

Her cry echoed up the bell tower, but until the bells rang on Sunday morning, no one would know what happened to Sister Mary Agnes.

CHAPTER TWO

Wednesday, October 22
TriMak Investigations

A T TWO MINUTES AFTER ten on Wednesday morning, the front door opened at the TriMak office, and a nun swooped in. Definitely old-school, decked out in a black dress with a cape, a white wimple cradling her wrinkled cheeks. I figured she was in costume since it was the week before Halloween.

I happened to be in the reception area talking to Germany Jones, our new office manager. Germany is twenty-three. His light brown hair fluffs out over his forehead. He's tall and on the skinny side, like a late adolescent who hasn't quite muscled up yet. Today he and I were dressed alike, in jeans and our blue TriMak polos.

Germany looked up. "Welcome to TriMak. How may we help you?" Very professional. Just the way I taught him.

The nun, unsmiling, rapped her knuckles on the counter in front of Germany's desk. "I need to see Erwin Bronson. Now."

I had the feeling she was the real deal. I never went to Catholic school, but I'd heard stories about strict nuns, and when you're a kid, stories about rulers on knuckles leave an impression. Something in her tone—commanding, demanding—made me wince.

Germany shot me a look, wide-eyed. He'd heard the stories too, evidently.

I stepped in. "I'll see if he's here, Sister—?"

She pulled herself up to full height—all five-foot-six of her. Shoulders back, chin up, she said, "I am Sister Celeste Marie— Mother Superior at Holy Assumption."

Superior, indeed. I turned and hurried to Chief Bronson's domain at the back of the TriMak office. I knocked on the door frame, and he looked up from his desk. "What's up, Chickie?"

The chief started calling me Chickie a while back because, in his words, I get "madder than a wet hen," and I fight "like a banty rooster." I hated the nickname at first. Now I like it. But I'm not going to tell him that.

"You have a visitor, Chief. A nun. Sister Celeste Marie?"

The chief—in his sixties, retired chief of the Three Rivers Police Department, strong, confident, no-nonsense Chief— paled. "She's here? Now?" He jumped out of his chair. "Don't keep her waiting!"

He raced past me. I followed him out to the reception area, got there just in time to hear her say, "Erwin. So nice to see you again."

"You too, Sister," he said, nodding his head a bunch of times, almost bowing. What's the word? Obsequious? Deferential? Scared? Hard to say. He led her back to his office and closed the door.

I raised an eyebrow at Germany. "'Erwin'? Nobody calls him that."

"She does, obviously."

"Maybe they have history since the chief graduated from Holy Assumption High. I wonder what she wants."

A minute later, the chief returned to the reception area. "Mack, can you come to my office, please?"

I followed him with the vague sense that I was in trouble. Like being called to the principal's office. I blamed it on the nun.

Sister Celeste Marie sat ramrod straight on one of the two chairs in front of the chief's desk, hands folded on her lap. I took the other chair as the chief introduced us.

Sister Celeste Marie eyed me up and down, frowning. "Rather young and inexperienced, isn't she, Erwin?"

I bristled. At thirty-five, I'm hardly a kid. And she had no idea who I was, what I'd been through. No idea of how I'd almost been shot, almost burned in my apartment and then in a cornfield. Almost drowned in a urinal. I'd been choked, hit with a brick, and attacked with a crockpot. I'd come close to having my skull cracked with a hatchet, and, most recently, I'd almost been tossed off a cliff. I'd survived all that while solving several cases in the last few months—and doing so brilliantly, if I do say so myself.

And now that I was officially licensed by the state, I was ready to tackle any case that came my way.

Sister Celeste had no idea, but Chief Bronson did. He smiled at me, then at her. "Mackenzie here is the perfect person to work with me on this case. I have absolute confidence she's the right choice."

"I suppose I must defer to your judgment, Erwin. I have no other options."

Not exactly a resounding vote of confidence. The chief said, "Mack, a member of the Holy Assumption convent has died, and Sister Celeste is asking us to check into it, to see if the police missed anything." He turned to her. "I have to ask, Sister," he said, his face softening and gentleness in his voice. "Is there any reason to think this might have been suicide?"

She stiffened. "Absolutely not! Unthinkable! And I told the police that, though I'm not sure they believed me."

The chief nodded. "I believe you, Sister." He turned to me. "Mack, since there's evidently no risk to the public, the cops will have closed the case. Or at least they'll have put it on the back burner."

Sister Celeste huffed. "Back burner? They've taken it off the stove entirely! Case closed!" She frowned at me, then at Chief Bronson, then gave a quick nod. "I have no choice but to defer to you in this matter. You'll keep me apprised of your progress." An order, not a request.

"Yes, Sister," the chief said.

Sister Celeste Marie stood. The chief stood. I stood.

She nodded at the chief, at me, then turned and swooshed out of the office. I closed the door behind her and returned to my seat.

I looked at the chief. "Erwin? I've never heard anyone call you Erwin."

He frowned. "And you won't. Chief or CB—that's who I am. Erwin is, uh, who I was, once upon a time."

I tried to picture a teenage Erwin, bopping around the halls of Holy Assumption High. Did young Erwin play sports? Was he in the band? Was he a popular kid? A nerd?

I met him when he was Chief Bronson of Three Rivers PD, when my late ex-husband, Billy, worked there. The chief retired a year ago and became a partner in TriMak Investigations with me and my former boss, Trip Kipling. The name TriMak is a combo of our two names, Trip and Mack. And with the chief, we are three equal partners.

A few months back, Sheena Shay—former cop turned private investigator—and her assistant, Germany Jones, came from The City (local shorthand for the metropolitan area an hour from Three Rivers) to work with us on a case. They joined the TriMak team—temporarily, we thought—but lately the whole arrangement seemed a lot more permanent.

I put my elbows on his desk. "So, Chief, what have we got?"

He leaned back, interlacing his fingers across his stomach. No sign of a paunch on the chief. He's in great shape at sixty-one. "What we have is a dead nun."

I sat back in my chair. "But it's a police matter, right?" I'd been warned a dozen times, by the chief, by Trip, and by Detective Heather Sullivan—my primary police contact—to keep my nose out of police matters.

"It was, but the cops are calling it an accidental death. They interviewed everybody and came up empty. Case closed."

"What do you think?" I asked.

He shrugged. "Maybe accidental, maybe not. Regardless, Sister Celeste wants to know for sure." He lowered his voice and leaned forward on his elbows, tenting his fingers. "She's worried it was someone on the inside."

My eyes went wide. "Like a nun? A *murdering* nun?"

He nodded. "If it is, she wants to keep it all quiet."

"How are we going to get access?"

He smiled. "Well, here's the part you're gonna love. You and me, Chickie—we're going undercover."

CHAPTER THREE

M Y JAW DROPPED. "UNDERCOVER? At Holy Assumption?" The church, convent, and high school occupied several blocks of southside real estate in Three Rivers.

Chief Bronson nodded. "Yep. You and me. Undercover."

"At the convent.

"Yep."

"Me. A nun." My voice squeaked a little.

The whole idea was far-fetched to say the least. I was raised loosey-goosey Lutheran. My mother tried to corral us five kids on Sunday mornings to get to Our Savior's—my grandmother's church—but most of the time, my single-mother mom was too tired from working to support us.

He laughed. "Yep. You'll be a nun, and I'm gonna be a priest."

Okay, even more far-fetched. I asked, "When are we doing this?"

"The funeral was yesterday. Sister Celeste suggested we come next Sunday afternoon, after things have settled down.

We'll spend next week there, or as long as the investigation takes. Oh, and by the way, you'll be teaching."

I got serious. "Teaching? High school students?" I took a deep breath. "What will I be teaching exactly?"

"You'll pick up where the, uh, deceased left off. Biology and hygiene."

I wrinkled my nose. "Great. Science isn't my strong suit. And biology class wasn't my favorite. All those dead frogs splayed out and stinking of formaldehyde. And hygiene? Talking to high schoolers about sex? As I recall, those classes involved a lot of snickering and rude drawings of body parts when the teacher wasn't looking."

He laughed. "You'll figure it out, I'm sure." His laptop dinged. "Hang on, Mack. I have to answer this email."

While he worked, I thought. *Teaching sex ed?* I hadn't had any personal experience in that area for longer than I care to admit. I'd been married to Billy, so I knew which end was up, so to speak, but lately—well, I was in a serious dry spell.

I was sort of dating two guys at the moment, but nothing serious was happening. I'd known Nick Milcross since high school, where he was cool and I was, um, less than cool. The girls adored him, and the boys admired him. He's tall, just over six feet, and athletic, with wavy brown hair and velvety brown eyes. Smells like sawdust and Old Spice. Nick's a real sweetie. And he has dimples.

And then there's Vince Hampton. Friend of my older brother Greg's, Vince was my middle school crush. He's a Three Rivers firefighter, incredibly fit at five-eleven, with dark hair and dark eyes. You might even say "smoldering good looks" if that wasn't such a pathetic pun for a firefighter. Vince is a bit of a bad boy who smells like smoke and bourbon.

Which one did I really want? Both. *Do we have to choose?*

I'd been quiet for a long time when the chief cleared his throat. "Earth to Chickie," he said.

I gave my head a quick shake to clear it. *Back to the case.* "Okay, so if I have to teach, I assume there are lesson plans? I mean, I don't have to just make stuff up, right?" My stomach did a flip. "And what am I supposed to wear?" I waved a hand over my blue TriMak polo shirt and jeans. "I don't have any nun clothes in my closet."

He chuckled. "Sister Celeste will provide what you need. And my cousin Benedict is a priest. He'll hook me up with whatever I need. So what do you say, Chickie? You game?"

"Do I have a choice?"

"Nope," he said.

When the chief says "do," you do. He's like my grandmother in that regard. The chief isn't my boss, but he has this air of no-nonsense authority. It's easier to just say yes to him right up front. You'll end up doing what he says anyway.

I let out a sigh. "Okay. Let's do it."

"I knew I could count on you, Chickie." He smiled.

CHAPTER FOUR

LEFT THE CHIEF AND crossed the hall to my office. Did I say "office"? Oops. I meant broom closet. Storeroom. Yup. This is where Mackenzie Prentice, Official Investigator, is housed these days. The storeroom.

I figured I'd have the middle of the three real offices at TriMak once my official investigator's license came through. Trip has the one in front, and the chief has the back office. But before my license came through, Sheena Shay, Big City Detective, showed up and took the middle office.

So when I was finally officially licensed and I gave Germany my job as office manager/receptionist, there was no room left at the inn, and the only space was the storeroom. Oh, I've had moments where I've fussed and fumed—to Gram, my friends—that maybe I should just set up my own investigation agency. Mack Prentice, Rogue Detective. Or Free Spirit. Or something like that.

But then Rational Me remembers that I have very little

experience, and being on my own means no backup, and I really do like working with Trip and the chief and Germany.

But Sheena? Not so much. She's a pushy, abrasive, know-it-all who constantly reminds me that she thinks Three Rivers is beyond Podunk. Not at all like the real world, meaning the Big City.

I know it's not fair that I, equal partner to Trip and the chief, am stuck in the storage closet. But Trip keeps assuring me that Sheena is only here in Three Rivers temporarily, and when she leaves, the middle office will be mine.

Anxious Me worries about that plan. *What if she never leaves? What if she and Trip end up living happily ever after? Blech. We'll be stuck in the closet forever.*

I brought that up to Trip, and he assured me that if Sheena decides to stay with us permanently, he will move us all to larger quarters in town. Then he asked if I would *please, please, please* just use the storeroom—temporarily.

The chief stays out of the whole thing. He's no doubt sick of arbitrating workplace squabbles after all those years as chief of police. He sounds like a dad when he says, "Figure it out, kids."

Kids? I'm over thirty, and Trip is in his forties. But I admit we can both be childish at times.

Speaking of children, I agreed to use the storeroom because I'm a middle child, and that means I'm a cooperator. *You mean a sucker*, says Snarky Me.

The storeroom was pretty empty to begin with. A broom, mop, and bucket. Some old boxes of stuff on a set of metal shelves. I cleaned out the junk and washed away the cobwebs and grime. Trip brought a small desk from his house and stuck it against one wall.

The ceiling light is a bare bulb in a white porcelain socket, with a chain you pull to turn the light on. The socket has an outlet built in, so there's an orange, heavy-duty extension cord plugged in at the ceiling that runs down the wall and over to my desk. A power strip is on the desk for my laptop and a lamp Gram gave me. I added one of those little coffee warmers too.

I'd add a plant, but it wouldn't last long.

I insisted on a really nice ergonomic chair that cost Trip a hefty chunk of change. I could have gotten by without the chair, but I deserved it for letting Sheena use my *real* office. Rational Me suggested I was being a little passive-aggressive, insisting on the expensive chair, but a girl's gotta do what a girl's gotta do, am I right?

I put a picture of Wonder Woman on the wall above my desk. "Wonder Chickie" is my official nickname around the office, but a picture of a chicken in a Wonder Woman suit does not appeal.

My friend Tansy gave me a metal sculpture of a chicken, about five inches tall. This chicken looks fierce, and angry, metal wings fully extended and head thrown back, its beak wide open. You can almost hear her squawking. I love the chicken— it exudes just the right combination of wickedness and whimsy.

My friend Jade, the artist, painted a small sign for me—a collaged background with the words, "This is not your whole story—just the next chapter."

Between the fierce chicken and the sign, I have hope. I won't be working out of a broom closet my whole life. It's not forever, just for now. Better days are coming. Right? Right.

I sat at my desk and opened my laptop. This is what I do when I have a new case. Start a file. Make my notes. What to call it? "Dead Nun" seemed awfully cold.

I decided it would be more professional to call it "Holy Assumption."

Germany spoke from my doorway. "Want a coffee, Mack?"

"Sure," I said. When we opened TriMak, I made sure everyone understood that we all make our own coffee. But if someone offers, what can we say?

A few minutes later, Germany returned with two cups of vanilla hazelnut, opened the folding chair I keep in the corner for visitors, and sat next to my desk. "Can I talk to you?"

"Sure, Germ. What's up?"

"Um, Trip and Sheena are getting, um . . ." He blushed and trailed off.

"Getting more obnoxious? More disgusting? More revolting? Shall I go on?"

Germany laughed. "All of the above." Germany and Sheena had been staying at Trip's house since they came to town. Sheena and Trip have a hot and heavy romance-thing going. It started the moment they laid eyes on each other.

He continued. "Three's a crowd, you know? I can tell they're annoyed that I'm around. It's time for me to get my own place."

"Can you afford it?" I knew what we were paying him at TriMak. And rents in Three Rivers have gone sky-high since a local-boy-made-good had decided to move his high-tech business to town. Attracting a lot of new, well-paid young professionals, and along with that, a high demand for apartment housing, and with that, new development, and, of course, higher rents. Simple economics. Supply and demand. What the market will bear, as the saying goes.

He shrugged. "Not sure what I'll be able to afford. I haven't really started looking. I thought maybe you could give me some direction since you've lived here so long."

"*So long*? How old do you think I am?"

He laughed. "I just mean your family is from here." He blushed again. *Sweet kid.*

"I can ask around," I said.

Coffee gone, Germany stood to leave as he asked, "So what was the nun's deal?"

I filled him in on the case.

Eyes wide, he said, "Undercover? Cool!"

I admit I love having Germany admire me, having him think I'm cool. I shrugged. "Nah. Just part of the job, kid. Just part of the job."

CHAPTER FIVE

ONE OF THE FIRST things I wanted to do was talk to my police connection and sort-of friend Heather Sullivan. She'd worked with (and slept with) my ex-husband, Billy, when he worked for the Three Rivers Police Department. Heather and I have since patched things up, and she is my go-to person for all things police-related. She also lets me know, in no uncertain terms, when I'm going too far or stepping on official toes in investigations.

Heather okayed a visit via text and was at her desk when I got there.

We're both in our mid-thirties and about the same height, though she's just a tad taller than my five-foot-six. There, the physical similarities end. She's gorgeous. I'm okay looking. She's got blonde hair, pulled this morning into a spun-gold ponytail. I've got mousy brown hair, barely long enough to pull back, with a few too-soon-to-have-them grays. She looked incredible in her navy jacket, slacks, and crisp white blouse.

She was in a jolly mood. "Hey Mack, have a seat." I sat in the chair in front of her desk.

Heather grinned at me, and I swear her teeth glinted in the office light.

"Why are you so happy?"

She smiled bigger. "Guess."

"Um, promotion?" She'd already made detective. What was next? "Got a raise?"

She shook her head. Her cornflower blue eyes twinkled.

I knew that look. "Aha! You've got a new guy."

She grinned, her cheeks flushing as she nodded. "And he's amazing."

"Anyone I know?" I knew some of the department people from the old days and from recent interactions.

She shook her head. "Nope. He's not from around here. He lives in The City." She told me they'd connected online on Mucho Matches and had been texting and chatting for a couple weeks. They hadn't yet had an in-person date. "He works most weekends," Heather said. "He's an attorney."

"An attorney who works weekends? You sure he's not 'working weekends'—I air-quoted—"because he's married?"

She gave me a look. "Duh. You think I didn't check him out? Divorced last year. Attorney in good standing, Good credit. New car. No red flags."

I held up my hands. "Okay, okay. I'm sure he's wonderful."

"We'll see. He's coming over here on Tuesday night. We're having dinner at Donatello's and then whatever."

"Well, congrats. I hope it goes well."

"So do I. But can I ask a big favor?"

"Sure."

"I don't want the department gossiping about this. Would you be willing to be my backup on Tuesday night, in the highly unlikely event that he turns out to be a jerk?"

Heather asking a favor meant she'd owe me one in the future. "No problem. Just text me if you need an out. I'll be at the convent."

Her jaw went slack. "At the convent? Seriously?"

"Yup. I'm going undercover as a nun."

"You. A nun." She tried not to laugh. "Do you even know anything about nuns? You aren't even Catholic, are you? Do you even go to church?"

"I'll definitely be a fish out of water. But the Mother Superior will help me. The chief and I will meet with her on Sunday afternoon. We'll be investigating the nun's death, and he thought it would be great if I went undercover."

"I assume you're talking about Holy Assumption and the nun who was found dead last Sunday?"

"Yes, that's the case. Any thoughts?"

She shrugged. "Accidental death. Case closed."

"What if it wasn't an accident?"

She shook her head. "Nope. We interviewed everybody. The old nun fell in the bell tower. She had bad knees. She hit her head on the concrete, going down. No reason to suspect anyone did her in."

"So if you've closed the case, you have no problem with me doing some checking."

"Why would you want to? Why waste your time with it?" She raised an eyebrow and smirked. "No other lost birds lately?"

My cheeks got hot. Heather knew about one of my earlier cases, with the little girl whose parakeet flew away. Fortunately, the girl's mother reported that Banjo the bird "came back on his own." *Wink, wink.*

I cleared my throat. "Very funny. The chief wants us to do some digging. See if you missed something." *Take that, wink, wink.* "The Mother Superior is an old friend of his."

Heather sat up in her chair. The chief had been her boss until he retired. "Well, if Chief Bronson is hands-on, the department will cooperate in any way we can. Let him know that, okay?"

"Okay. So does that mean I can have a copy of the report?"

"Public record. But I'll get you a copy, personally." Heather was being uncharacteristically nice.

I narrowed my eyes. "What's the deal? Why are you being so helpful?"

She chuckled. "I don't blame you for being skeptical, given our history." She and I had butted heads on more than one occasion. "I'm working toward my next promotion, and Chief Bronson and Chief Wardell are golfing buddies. I figure it won't hurt if my former boss tells my current boss how helpful I can be to our community members."

Whatever worked. She tapped keys on her laptop and a minute later, pulled several pages off her printer and handed them to me. "Here you go."

The full report. Just like that. "Thanks, Detective Sullivan. I'll let you know if I have any questions."

"You do that. I'm always happy to help." She shot me a huge smile.

I left, wondering how long this kinder, gentler Detective Sullivan would stick around.

CHAPTER SIX

HEADED HOME AFTER WORK on Wednesday. Gram and my mother were in the kitchen, making dinner. Gram was elbow-deep in raw meat, mixing meatloaf in her big ceramic bowl. My mouth watered. Gram makes the best meatloaf in the history of meatloaf. My mother was at the sink, peeling potatoes.

I filled them in on the plan. "I'll be staying in the convent at Holy Assumption until we figure out what happened. Gram, could you take care of Chloe and the birds?" My parakeets, Tweet and Chirp, fellow survivors of my apartment fire, live in Gram's front parlor, where the big windows offer a view of their outdoor friends. Chloe the cat was displaced by the fire as well and adopted me as her human.

Gram said, "No problem, sweetie. How interesting for you to be staying at the convent!"

"Yup. I'll be undercover. As one of the sisters." I waited for my mother's reaction.

She did not disappoint. She snorted. "You? A nun? Ha! How you gonna pull *that* off?"

"Not a nun. A *sister*."

"What's the difference?"

"The chief told me that nuns are more separated from the world and spend a lot of time praying."

My mother laughed. "Well, that's definitely not you!"

"Agreed. A 'sister,' on the other hand, spends more time serving the community where she is, uh . . ."—I tried to remember what the chief had said—"where she's stationed."

My mother said, "Sounds like being in the military."

Gram smiled. "Well, they are in God's army, aren't they? I love the idea that people dedicate themselves to living out their faith like that."

Gram has dedicated her life to encouraging her family, especially her grandchildren to, as she put it, "keep the faith." Some have; some haven't. Brother Greg and his family attend Redeemer Lutheran in town, and his oldest, Joey, is doing confirmation classes. Sister Deanne and her family go to her husband's family's church—Methodist, I think—in LaCroix, a town two hours south of Three Rivers, where they live.

My younger brother Robbie is single in LA, living a bachelor's life. Never mentions a church. And my older sister Stephanie—big city investment adviser—seems to worship money.

For me, I'm kind of in the middle, as I often am. Not too much, not too little. I'll go to Our Savior's with Gram on occasion. I believe there is something out there, something or someone watching over us all. But I'm not committed to calling that whatever anything in particular. God, Universe, Higher Power. I don't pretend to know for sure. But there is *some*thing. I am sure of that.

My mother set down the potato peeler and wiped her hands on a dish towel with a row of little yellow chicks across the bottom edge. (Gram is crazy about chickens.) "Do you have to wear a habit? *That* I'd like to see."

"Nuns or sisters wear anything these days, but I'll probably be wearing—" I didn't want to say that I might be wearing the dead nun's clothes. "Um, clothes will be provided."

Gram got excited. "Ooh, one of those Flying Nun get-ups? I loved that show! That cute little Sally Field with that big hat!" She swooped both her arms out from the meatloaf mix.

Unfortunately my mother was right in the line of fire. Gram's right hand smacked my mother's cheek and left behind a blob of hamburger. A goopy hunk of onion landed in my mother's hair.

My mom yelped. "Ow! Mother! Watch where you're flying!"

Gram said, "Sorry, hon. I go where the wind takes me!"

My mother sat at the table, wiped the meatloaf off her cheek with the chicken dish towel. "That hurt, Ma! You probably gave me a black eye."

Gram leaned in to inspect the red spot on my mother's cheek, then picked the hunk of onion out of her hair. She went to the freezer, then handed my mom a bag of frozen vegetables. "I'm so sorry, hon. This will help."

My mother looked at it. "Frozen okra? Who the heck eats okra around here?"

Gram shrugged. "I saw a recipe on the cooking channel and thought it sounded good. But I never made it." She turned to me. "So Mackenzie, what do you think you'll wear?"

"Well, nobody wears those flying nun hats these days." I said that like I knew what I was talking about, but, of course, there might be nuns in the world who dressed just that way. To be honest, I thought it would be cool if I could.

Gram looked a little disappointed. "Too bad. That would be a hoot!"

"I guess I'll just wear a skirt and blouse. Probably subdued colors."

My mother gave another snort. "Ha! You in a skirt? When is the last time you wore anything besides jeans?"

I looked down at my outfit. "This is my work uniform. And I love jeans."

My mom pressed the okra against her cheek, stood, and headed upstairs. "I'm going to go lie down until dinner. It's dangerous in this kitchen."

"You do that, dear. You need a rest," Gram said as she lifted the meat mixture from the bowl and plopped it into a loaf pan. She shaped the meatloaf, then pressed an indent along the top with the side of her hand. She filled the indent with a squiggle of ketchup, then laid pieces of raw bacon over it. As she put the pan in the oven, she asked, "So how long will you be a nun, or a sister, or whatever?"

"The chief figures we'll be undercover a week, maybe less. Depends on how fast we finish our investigation."

Gram's blue eyes twinkled. "Ooh, I love an investigation! What's the case?"

"Gram, you know this is confidential. This is TriMak business, and I don't need you and Velma getting involved." Gram and her friend Velma had interfered in cases in the past. "And besides, you might worry about me, and I don't want that. You have enough to worry about."

Gram's third husband is Nathan—in his eighties, like Gram is, and he is, as he puts it, "losing my marbles." Gram has gradually taken on his daily care. "A blessing and a burden" is how she describes caregiving.

Gram said, "I'll worry more imagining the worst."

I thought about that. "Okay, but you can't tell anyone else. Promise?"

She held up her right hand. "I promise. Cross my heart." She drew a cross on her chest with her left hand.

Gram and I stood at the sink, dicing the potatoes my mother had peeled and putting them in a pot of salted water. I told her about Sister Mary Agnes and how the chief and I would be undercover trying to see if this was, as Mother Superior feared, an inside job.

"Velma's kids went to Holy Assumption."

"Gram, you can't say anything about this to Velma or any of your other friends." Gram and her friends know everything about everybody in Three Rivers.

"I won't. But I'll bet Velma knew this Mary Agnes. And she told me about all the tunnels. Tunnels connecting the church and the school. She said her kids told her how they'd skip class and hide out down there and smoke." She lowered her voice, adding in a half-whisper. "She said the kids call the school 'Holy Ass.' Isn't that awful? So disrespectful."

I gave a shrug. "Yeah, kids. What can you do?"

The potatoes diced, we dried our hands on other chicken-decorated dishtowels. Gram put the potatoes on the stove.

I turned her toward me and took hold of both her upper arms. I said, in as stern a tone as I could muster, "Gram, you can't talk to Velma about this case. Understand? You cannot— repeat, cannot—say one word to her. Understand?"

Gram nodded.

"Pinky swear?"

We locked pinkies, and then she made that little lip-locking motion with her fingers. But I knew from past experience that we could pinky swear and lip-lock all day long, and that still didn't guarantee her silence.

CHAPTER SEVEN

I ATE MY FILL OF meatloaf and mashed potatoes, with apple pie and ice cream for dessert. Gram and Nathan relaxed in the family room, watching *Wheel of Fortune*, while my mother washed the dishes and I dried.

My mom leaned toward me. "Can you tell where Gram hit me? I'm going to have a black eye. I just know it."

I peered at her cheek. "Just the slightest spot of pink right there." I touched the spot, and she winced. *Drama queen.*

The kitchen clean, my mother left for her boyfriend Duncan's house. I thanked Gram for dinner, hugged her and Nathan, said goodnight, and went to the carriage house.

I poured a glass of Wollersheim Prairie Sunburst and brought it, the police report, and a pen and paper notepad to my dining table. Pen and paper. Old school. I think best when I can actually write things down, see things before me in black and white.

Chloe rubbed against my leg before curling herself at my feet. "Well, girl, let's dig into this thing," I said. She closed her eyes.

Reading a death investigation report always gives me pause. The end of a life summed up so clinically. Cold, hard facts of life. Of death.

DECEASED: Clara Ann Conrad, aka Sister Mary Agnes. AGE: 77. The address and phone number listed were Holy Assumption's.

DECEASED FOUND BY: Sister Bernadette Clark. DATE AND TIME FOUND: Sunday, October 20th at 7:55 a.m. LAST SEEN BY: Sister Petronilla. I jotted a note to talk with both of them.

CONDITION OF BODY: This part of a death investigation report always gives me the willies, thinking about what happens to our bodies after death. Words like "rigor" and "lividity" don't come up in polite conversation.

In the case of Sister Mary Agnes, her body was "cool" and "clean." The report indicated that some dried blood was present at the scene, around her body and a small amount on the stairs here and there. Consistent with taking a header down a flight of concrete steps.

The next question: "Was this death related to domestic violence?" Answer: No. You think of domestic violence between intimate partners, right? But that stuff can happen in any family. Even a community of religious sisters? Seemed highly unlikely, but you never know.

FIRST OFFICER ON SCENE: Samantha Dutton. I know Officer Dutton from past, um, what shall I call them? "Adventures in detectiving"? "Close encounters of the investigatory kind"? The truth: She and I had spent time in a landfill together. I made a note to talk with Dutton.

NEXT OF KIN: Anna Conrad Marberry, sister to the sister. That had to be confusing. Her address was a senior living facility in Proctor Falls.

I needed to talk with Officer Dutton and this Anna Marberry, hopefully before going undercover. *Gather background information.* Rational Me has some valuable investigatory skills.

DESCRIPTION OF SCENE: The bell tower at Holy Assumption had concrete stairs, walls, floor. Just what you'd expect. The kind of thing you see on television.

I made a note: Check out BELL TOWER.

So far, the police report revealed nothing but a dead nun at the base of a concrete staircase. Under FORENSIC EVIDENCE: no weapons, ligatures, blunt objects. No firearms or ammo. No vehicle, no blood spatter. No notes or letters. No latent prints. No evidence of alcohol, but under drugs, a note indicated a prescription for gabapentin.

I'd never heard of that one. Google to the rescue. Gabapentin was prescribed for nerve pain but also to help manage arthritis pain. "Particularly for knee osteoarthritis." That certainly fit. Side effects could be "loss of balance, unsteadiness, dizziness." Possibly fit. Also, "trouble with thinking." Had she gotten confused? Was she hearing things? Imagining things?

Suicidal thoughts might be an issue for "a small number of people," Google said. Did that apply to Sister Mary Agnes? Did she climb those stairs to toss herself out of the bell tower?

The next section indicated Sister Mary Agnes was fully clothed—blouse, skirt, cardigan. Underclothing in place, thank goodness. Silver chain with a cross and a rosary noted under JEWELRY.

WOUNDS: Abrasions and contusions.

MANNER OF DEATH: Head trauma and notes "injuries consistent with a fall down stairs. Possible skull fracture." Ouch.

SUSPECTED CAUSE: The box for "accidental" was checked.

Photos had been taken by Officer Dutton. Personal effects released to Sister Celeste Marie at Holy Assumption.

The scene diagram, where Dutton, or maybe another officer, sketched the position of her body, offered limited detail. I turned to the body outlines at the back of the report. Notes on that page were made by a G. Finlay, MD. Most likely a doctor at Our Lady of Mercy. I'd have to ask Dutton.

Circles on the head, knees, arms, legs indicated "contusion" and "ecchymosis"—a fancy word for bruises, according to my Google friends. On the left wrist and on the head: "possible fracture." Double ouch.

"Okay, Chloe," I said, and she looked up as I stood. Sometimes it helps me to think out loud and try to reenact the scene. "This Mary Agnes goes up the stairs. Why? We don't know." I walked toward the stairs leading to my bedroom loft and took several steps upward. "Somewhere on the stairs, she loses her balance." I pinwheeled my arms. "Maybe she slips. Maybe her hip gives out. Or her knee. She loses her balance and goes backward down the steps."

I backed down the stairs, flailing my arms, twisting, grabbing for the railing. I pictured TV scenes where people fall down the stairs. The slo-mo roll down curved staircases in fancy houses. The slip-and-fall down a wooden basement staircase, usually after the bad guy has sawn partway through one of the boards.

I missed the bottom step and stumbled toward the cat. She gave a yowl and jumped clear.

"Sorry, girl!"

Chloe took off for parts unknown. I sat back at the table, talking to myself. "Maybe Sister Mary Agnes missed a step. Was it dark in that tower?" I made more notes: What time? Check stairs same time of day.

I could imagine how it might have happened, but why was she up there to begin with? She was on cleaning duty, Sister Celeste Marie had told us at TriMak. Did the bells need dusting?

Rational Me thought not. Anxious Me wondered if Sister Mary Agnes was a compulsive cleaner. Little-Bit-of-OCD Me likes things to be neat and orderly. "Clean and pristine," I call it. Maybe the good sister thought it her duty to clean things nobody ever sees.

I get that. I take great pride in having my bathroom vanity drawers neat and tidy. And same with my utensil drawers in the kitchen. My mother is the same way and taught the five of us that things needed to be clean and orderly, "just in case."

Just in case somebody drops in. Just in case you have company and they go into your bathroom and snoop in your drawers. If my friends decide to snoop, they will find my things in order. But I'm not fanatical about it. Ninety-nine percent clean is good enough for me.

I blinked my eyes and yawned. The details of the report were getting fuzzy in my mind. I'd had a big dinner, dessert, and two glasses of wine. I was done for the night.

It was after 10:00 p.m. when I tucked the report back into its envelope, put my wine glass in the sink, turned off the lights, and headed up to my bed in the carriage house loft. Chloe was waiting for me, flanked out on my duvet.

She purred me to sleep.

CHAPTER EIGHT

I GOT UP EARLY ON Thursday, ready to review the police report again. I made coffee and a couple pieces of toast with peanut butter and brought them to my table. I'd just taken the report out of the envelope when someone knocked. Clayton—one of Nick's construction guys—and a helper were at the door.

Last summer, part of the maple tree behind the carriage house had come crashing down in a thunderstorm, through the roof, flooding the upstairs bedroom loft and the bathroom downstairs. Nick and his crew had made the repairs, but a recent heavy rain had made us all aware that the roof wasn't quite watertight. Certainly not flooding, but a pesky leak in the ceiling near my closet. Nick said he'd take care of it before I had to start bunking on the couch downstairs.

Maybe he has an ulterior motive in wanting the bedroom available, Lonely Me hoped.

While Clayton and his helper banged away upstairs, I re-read the police report and reviewed my notes. "Bell tower stairs. Why? What time?" I had several people on my "talk to" list. Too soon to guess who'd be moving to the "suspects" list.

I got up to refill my coffee cup when Clayton hollered for me to come up to the loft. I climbed the stairs and let out a gasp. Several feet of the roof at the far end of the loft had been stripped down to the joists. A huge ball of soggy insulation was stuffed into a plastic bag near my closet.

Clayton said, "Sorry, but this is worse than we thought. We've found the source of the leak, but as you can see, we'll have to replace everything on that end. We can tarp it, but it might be a couple days before we're finished. It's going to be cold up here at night. You have somewhere else you can sleep?"

Not again! I wanted to scream, but I stifled myself. The Rose Room at Gram's, where I'd stayed after the apartment fire and during the carriage house renovation, felt like a big step backward.

I had other options. My couch, of course. Or I could have stayed with a friend—Tansy has a guest room, and Jade and her dad have a whole house.

And either Nick or Vince would be glad to have a sleepover with me—at least Lonely Me hoped so—but since I wasn't sure which one of them I really wanted, I didn't want to start something I might later regret.

"No problem sleeping on the couch," I told Clayton. "Thanks for taking care of this."

He gave me a little salute as I headed back downstairs.

Rational Me had assured him it wasn't a problem to vacate my bedroom. *What choice do we have but to accept and adapt to the situation?* Rational Me sounds like my yoga-guru friend, Tansy. She's into all that mindfulness stuff.

Lonely Me sighed. *I guess our love life can wait.*

As I went back to the kitchen table, Snarky said, *Why wait? Who needs a bedroom? People do it in cars, on couches. On kitchen tables, for goodness' sake.*

Rational Me reminded her that I was too old to be doing it in cars.

Anxious said, *And for sure not on the kitchen table! People eat there!*

Snarky called her a prude.

Rational Me weighed in. *Nothing wrong with waiting for the right place and the right time to get busy with the right somebody.*

Badass wasn't having it. *Anytime. Anywhere. Bring it.*

I left them arguing and headed for TriMak.

Half an hour later, I was going to my broom closet at TriMak with a cup of coffee, when I turned to see Germany coming in the back door with somebody. Well, I thought it was a "somebody" and quickly realized it was a "something." A body. Headless.

The top half was stuffed into one of Trip's old shirts—an ugly plaid I recognized from long ago—with garden gloves pinned to the sleeves for hands. The bottom half of the body wore a pair of old jeans stuffed into boots.

I followed Germany to the front reception area, where he parked the body on one of the chairs. He topped it with a head.

"How'd you make the head?" I asked.

"Soccer ball in a pillowcase. And the body is stuffed with pillows and towels."

"Brilliant. Where's his face?"

Germany reached into a bag from the Dollar Store and pulled out a rubber mask of a recent president. He duct-taped it on the head and added a shaggy blond wig and a backward baseball cap.

"Hail to the chief," he said, laughing. I laughed with him.

Chief Bronson walked into the reception area. "What so funny?" he asked, saw the dummy, and got serious. He shook his head. "Nope! Not him! Absolutely not!" The chief is a stickler for respecting authority, regardless of who is in the position. "Find another face, Germany."

"Yes, sir," Germany said. "I brought an alternative." He took a clown mask from the bag. Not the fun-circus-for-kiddies kind of clown, but the clown-from-hell kind of face. Killer clown.

He replaced the president with the clown, trading the blond wig for a wild red one. He stuck the backward baseball cap on top, then crossed the fake legs at the knee and fixed the fake hands so it was holding a copy of *Guns and Ammo* from the reception area table.

He stood back, admiring his work. "Creepy, huh?"

I nodded. "Definitely creepy."

"Definitely an improvement," the chief said, then headed to his office. He called over his shoulder, "Mack, let's talk."

I followed him, closed his office door, and took the chair in front of his desk.

He said, "Give me an update." He commands. I obey.

"I've read the police report. I need to talk with Officer Dutton—she was first on the scene. And I'm going to drive to Proctor Falls to talk with the deceased's next of kin. The sister's sister lives there in a senior community. Anything else you can think of for me to do before we go to the convent on Sunday?"

"Good start, Chickie. I'll be heading to Rollo's cabin this afternoon. Hoping to bag some turkey." The chief's good friend Rollo Carson is a retired judge, and they've hunted and fished together for years. They'd had a falling out over the summer, but they'd patched things up recently. Judge Carson's cabin is a five-hour drive north from Three Rivers.

"I'll be back Sunday afternoon and will meet you at the convent. Three-ish. Sister Celeste will give us the tour. We can settle in, get a feel for the place, maybe start some interviews. Then on Monday, you'll start teaching."

I felt a flutter of anxiety at the thought of standing—exposed, vulnerable—in front of a roomful of teenagers. In this day and age, thanks to the internet, they probably knew more than I did about every subject.

"Makes me nervous," I confessed.

The chief waved a hand. "I'll be around for backup."

"I'm not worried about the case being dangerous. I'm worried about the teaching."

Again with a hand wave. "You'll be fine."

Easy for him to say. He's a retired cop. He has a commanding presence. I, on the other hand, am just a girl, really. Not a lot of wisdom. Certainly not commanding, no matter what Badass Me claims. And I've never been a cop. I am, at best, an accidental detective.

At 10:30 the team gathered in Trip's office for the TriMak weekly debrief. We usually meet on Fridays to review the week's events. Consulting with each other on cases. Planning for the upcoming week. Personal plans for the weekend. But since the chief was going hunting, we were meeting on Thursday instead.

Trip provides the jelly donuts—his favorite, raspberry-filled with white icing. He inevitably makes a mess with donut jelly. It's not a matter of "if" but "when and how much." This morning, he'd already gotten jelly on his left arm just opening the box.

Trip closed the office door when we were all seated. Germany started us off, saying he was settling in as our office manager. We all told him what a great job he was doing. He beamed.

The chief told us he'd closed an unsolved case for the Three Rivers PD. He loves attacking old cases from his days as police chief, cases with what he calls "unsatisfactory resolutions." He'd solved the case, then presented his findings, obtained from "unnamed sources," to Heather Sullivan, letting her take the credit. "She's going for a promotion, so I thought I'd help her out."

The chief is generous that way. I hoped Heather appreciated it.

Trip said his big win was attending a Lions Club meeting in Bartonville, a town thirty miles up the Wolf River from Three Rivers. He caught a glob of jelly before it hit his shirt, licked it off his finger, and set the donut down. "It was a big meeting. Lots of interest in what we're doing. Should get referrals from them."

Trip's primary function in the agency is marketing. He's good at the schmoozing.

I am not interested in schmoozing. I am only interested in solving the mysteries. So what if I get a little banged up in the process. I love it. L-O-V-E it!

"How is Sheena doing?" the chief asked.

Trip said, "She's fine. She's at my cabin, resting, relaxing." Trip's family has a cabin near Deerwood, an hour and a half north of Three Rivers.

The chief asked, "Any sign of those no-goods from The City who were after her?"

Trip shook his head. "Nope. And she's got Curly up there for protection." Trip had temporarily—reluctantly—adopted

Curly, the goldendoodle, when our upstairs renter, Ralph, had to go to the hospital. Curly is a big, lovable goofball of a dog—hardly one you'd look to for protection.

Ralph's dog Moe, the shar-pit, had come home with me, and the chief took Ralph's third dog, Larry, an old German shepherd mix. Ralph was still recovering at Drury's Rest on River Street, but he hoped to be back in his apartment soon. No doubt, Larry, Moe, and Curly would be thrilled to be back home with Ralph. They were his pack.

When my turn came, I filled the team in on my approach to the dead nun case. Then I couldn't resist saying it was a win for me that I hadn't torched the broom closet yet.

Germany laughed, Trip squirmed in his chair, and the chief remained stone-faced. I said, "It's no joke, you guys. I'm an officially licensed investigator now, and I'm stuck operating out of a broom closet. What does that say to any prospective clients I meet with?"

Trip screwed up his face and said, "It tells them that you are a patient, accommodating person."

"Ha! More like I'm at the bottom of the pecking order around here."

Germany snickered. "Heh, heh. Chickie. Pecking order. Get it?"

I slapped him on the arm.

Trip said, "Patience, Mack, patience. This will all work out. You'll see."

I gave a wave of my hand, controlling which fingers went up. I turned to Germany. "Can you take Moe while I'm at the convent?" Germany had already told the chief he'd take care of Larry for the week. "I'm sure Larry will be glad to see Moe."

Trip gave a low growl.

I said, "Hey, Trip, how fun for you to have Larry and Moe at your house. Maybe you and Sheena can reunite them with Curly."

Trip sneered. "Not funny. And the dogs are temporary. It's *all* very temporary."

I said, "Ha! That's what you keep saying about me working out of the broom closet."

"Well, that's differ—uh, I mean—" Trip stumbled over his words then dismissed the meeting.

CHAPTER NINE

G ERMANY AND I WERE alone in the office by noon on Thursday. The chief had taken off for his hunting weekend. Trip left after the morning meeting, probably headed to his cabin to protect Sheena from those big city "bad guys" she claimed were looking for her.

Snarky doubted there were any bad guys. *She's just using that excuse to stay here with Trip.* I ran that theory past Germany.

He said, "No, someone is definitely trying to get their hands on her."

"Like who? Pimps? Drug dealers? Mobsters? Who did she tick off?"

He shrugged. "I have no idea. All I know is that before we left The City to come here last summer, there were hang-ups on the office phone. She was sure someone was following her. She got super paranoid, even worried that somebody might blow up her car."

"That old rust-bucket she drove here?" Sheena had rolled into Three Rivers in an old green oil-burning Chevy station wagon, with no air conditioning and tires that once upon a time had tread. Hardly the vehicle a *successful* big-city detective would drive. The car had breathed its last a month ago, its transmission shot, and it was now parked behind the TriMak office.

"Yeah, she changed her routines, her schedule. Came in early one day, late the next, changing it at random. She told me she was driving different routes every day to the office. I never knew what to expect."

"Did you ever see anyone actually following her? Suspicious activity around the office? Strangers lurking about?"

He shook his head.

I was having serious doubts about the whole deal. "Germany, did anyone ever threaten *you*? I mean in some cases, the bad guys might grab someone close to the person they are after and hold them hostage."

His eyes got huge. "Seriously?" He shook his head. "Oh man, I could have been in real danger. Maybe I still am!" He grabbed my arm, eyes bigger, voice higher. "Do *you* think I still am?"

I patted his hand. "Relax, Germ. If they were after you, they'd have made a move by now." I left him fidgeting and looking out the front office window, muttering to himself.

I went to my broom—office—to make some calls. I left a voicemail for Lou Burgess to let her know I'd be busy the next week. Lou had hired me, part-time, to help her stay organized in her store—Lou's Vintage on River Street. Lou is a long-time friend of my grandmother's, and this is what we do in Three Rivers—we help each other when we can.

My next call was to Hidden Valley, the assisted living place in Proctor Falls, where Sister Mary Agnes's sister lived. I left a message, and she called back ten minutes later and agreed to meet with me that afternoon at two.

Before I headed to Proctor Falls, Germany and I walked to Java Java for lunch. We ordered hot turkey hoagies and sat in one of the high-backed booths overlooking River Street.

Our little town decorates River Street for the seasons. Orange and black Halloween decorations hung from the lampposts, and store windows along the street were decorated with pumpkins, witches, black cats, and white ghosts. In the days after Halloween, all of that would be replaced with sparkling snowflakes and white lights over the street, creating a twinkling tunnel of light, ready for the holidays.

"Three Rivers is a great town. What was it like growing up here?" Germany asked.

I spent the rest of the lunch hour recounting tales of the adventures I'd had with my four siblings.

"You had a great childhood," Germany said, a wistful tone in his voice. I knew he'd had just one sister who struggled with depression.

I said, "It must have been tough to have a sibling with issues."

He nodded. "Yeah, our parents spent all their time worrying about her. All the focus was on her." He gave a chuckle. "They're lucky I didn't start getting into trouble, just to get their attention."

I reached across the table and squeezed his arm. "I'm glad you chose wisely, Foghorn." Germany had given himself that nickname—after the cartoon rooster, Foghorn Leghorn, an appropriate sidekick to my Chickie. We're a great team. And Germany is a great kid.

I had an idea. I picked up my cell phone, sent a text, and a couple seconds later, got a reply. "Great news, Germany. My grandmother says you can stay at her house until you find a place." *Good ol' Gram.*

As we finished our hoagies, I told him about the Rose Room and all the perks he could expect. "Endless supply of cookies. Cinnamon rolls to die for. Melt-in-your-mouth desserts every night." My addiction to sugar might have come from Gram.

Germany grinned. "Seriously? Thank you so much!"

Magnanimous Me was proud.

We polished off our sodas, brought our trash to the bussing station, and headed back toward the office. A few doors down from TriMak, I noticed a car parked in front of the building.

Muscle car. Bright yellow. Camaro. Brother Greg had a red Camaro in high school. *Good job noticing details.*

A man—medium height, medium build with a little extra paunch in front, longish brown hair in back, probably worn long to compensate for the balding on top. In a calf-length black coat, he leaned on the hood of the car, smoking a cigarette and watching TriMak's front door.

My Spidey senses tingled. *Bad guy from The City looking for Sheena?*

I put out an arm to stop Germany and pulled him off the sidewalk into the recessed doorway of Gregerson Accounting. I pointed ahead. "Look at that guy. Does he look familiar?"

Germany stuck his head out of the doorway and squinted. "I don't recognize him, but I like the car."

"Have you seen that car before?"

He squinted harder. "I don't think so, but it looks like it's got out-of-state plates."

"Out of state, like from The City?"

"Maybe."

I peeked out. "Can't tell if he's alone. The windows are tinted. Let's take the alley and go in through the back door." We went inside, and I turned the deadbolt behind us. I paused in the kitchenette and peeked around the corner of the wall.

The guy was at the front door, shielding his eyes with his hands and peering through the glass. Maybe he'd noticed us coming in the back.

I sucked in a breath. "Don't move, Germany. Don't breathe."

We stood statue-still for what seemed like forever until I heard a car start. The driver revved the engine, and I recognized the loud growl of glass-pack mufflers. Just like Greg's. He'd been so proud of that car.

When I peeked back around the corner, man and Camaro were gone.

I exhaled loudly. "Whew! Good Lord," I said. "Who was that?"

Germany grabbed my arm. "You think they found us? You think it was one of them?"

I didn't want to say that it could have been one of Sheena's "bad guys" and that he might have been planning to snatch Germany, hoping to force Sheena to come forward.

Anxious Me was sure that was the case. Rational Me pooh-poohed the idea. *Just a client, that's all. Perfectly safe.* "He was probably just a potential client."

Germany wasn't convinced. "Client or not, I should get a gun, just in case."

I explained to him all the hoops he'd have to jump through to get a gun in our state, all the regulations and required training. By the time he was licensed to carry, the whole Sheena situation would probably be resolved.

"Okay, I can at least get some mace, right? Or pepper spray?"
I explained that there were rules about those things as well.
"Fine! I'll carry a jackknife then."

"No problem with that, as long as you're not planning to fly anywhere."

I invited Germany to come along to interview Mrs. Marberry. He declined, saying he had office manager stuff to do. I hated leaving him alone in the office, but he promised to keep the doors locked.

CHAPTER TEN

O N THE DRIVE SOUTH from Three Rivers toward Proctor Falls, the terrain changes from rolling farm fields to higher hills and cliffs as the highway follows the Wolf River. I love this time of year, when the late October sky is the bluest blue. The sun, brilliant through the bare trees, warmed the interior of Cricket as I drove.

I named my Ford Escape Cricket after I bought it from my brother Greg, whose children had left all kinds of interesting things in the car, the most interesting of which was a real live cricket. I call him Jimbo in honor of that most venerated of cartoon crickets, Jiminy. I feed Jimbo cricket food I buy on Amazon and the occasional snack. He's lived somewhere under the back seat for several months now. How long do crickets live? We'll see.

I said over my shoulder, "Gorgeous day, huh, Jimbo?" He chirped in agreement.

Fall colors—red, orange, yellow—had long since come and gone. The last of the cornfields were being shorn to stubble. In one field, the farmer had left a patch of several rows of corn-stalks standing, all the way down the middle of the field.

"A cornfield mohawk!" I laughed aloud, wishing Germany had come along to laugh with me. Jimbo has no sense of humor.

I arrived at the Hidden Valley Senior Living complex and walked toward the canopied main entrance. I followed the sign for OFFICE into the main building. A middle-aged man wearing a shirt with BRAD over one front pocket and HIDDEN VALLEY over the other was at the front desk. I introduced myself and asked for Anna Marberry as I slid my card toward him.

"TriMak Investigations? What's this about?"

"A private matter. If Mrs. Marberry wishes to discuss it with you, that's up to her."

I followed Brad to a lounge area with several leather couches, armchairs, and coffee tables. Through floor-to-ceiling windows, I watched a pair of cardinals and a chickadee visiting a bird feeder on a pole outside. Fancier birds—rose-breasted grosbeaks and orioles—spend summers here but had headed south after the first frost.

Beyond the feeders, benches and tables were scattered here and there. They'd soon be covered in snow. But on this warm October day, several residents mingled outside, having coffee at one table, playing cards at another. Enjoying autumn's last hurrah.

The whole place had the feel of a high-end hotel. *Mrs. Marberry must have some bucks,* I thought as I sank onto a sumptuous couch and waited. A few minutes later, a tanned, fit woman approached. Her gray hair was cut short. She wore running shoes—I recognized the pricey brand. Silver Power was embroidered on the oversized sweatshirt she wore over black leggings. As the nun's younger sister, she was probably in her early seventies, but she could have passed for mid-fifties, tops.

"Miss Prentice?" She extended a manicured hand. "Anna Marberry. Would you care for coffee? Or tea?"

"Coffee would be great," I said.

She waved to Brad, and he came over. "Two coffees, please, Brad."

"Right away, ma'am," he said and disappeared.

I looked around the large room, outfitted with high-end furnishings, tastefully arranged. "This is really nice," I said. "How long have you lived here?"

"Just over a year. I moved in shortly after my husband died."

"I'm so sorry for your loss," I said.

"Thank you. He was ill, in a great deal of pain. It's a difficult thing watching someone you love suffer like that. It was a blessing when his suffering ended. And I can't say I was sorry to leave our home after all of that. This has been a fresh start for me, a new beginning."

Brad returned with a tray holding two ceramic mugs, a carafe, a small pitcher of cream, and a small bowl with packets of sweeteners—the pink stuff, the blue stuff, and the real white stuff. He set the tray down on the coffee table and walked away. Anna Marberry poured coffee into the cups and added cream to hers. "You'd like to talk about my sister."

Getting right to it. Okay. "Yes." I picked up my cup. "Again, so sorry for your loss."

She took a sip of coffee and then leaned back, both palms wrapped around her mug. "The police were here, and I told them all I knew. My sister and I were not very close, I'm afraid. Different paths in life and all that."

I waited, sipping coffee. *Let them fill the silence.*

After a bit, Mrs. Marberry continued. "She was very upset with me when I married my husband. He was an atheist, and she just didn't understand how I could abandon my faith to marry him. I tried to tell her I hadn't abandoned God myself, but she just didn't understand. Every time we talked, I sensed tension whenever his name came up. I told her one day that we'd just have to agree to disagree and leave it at that."

I sipped my coffee as two other residents came in the door, laughing as they passed through the lounge. I waited until they were out of earshot. "When is the last time you saw your sister?"

Anna Marberry set her coffee on the table and looked up at the ceiling. *Do liars avoid eye contact? Not necessarily. People trying to remember look up too. Detectiving 101.*

"We had lunch last Saturday afternoon." Tears welled. She pressed her hands against her face, sniffed, cleared her throat, and looked at me. "If I'd just stayed . . ."

Seems genuine. Or is she just a very good actress?

Rational Me fumed. *What is wrong with you? Can't you see she's grieving? Not everyone is a suspect. She's a broken-hearted sister.* I had to admit that my short tenure in investigations was making me suspicious of everyone.

"I'm so sorry," I said. I gave her a moment, then said, "I know it must be difficult to talk about all this, but the police assume that she fell, that her death was accidental. What do you think?"

"Clara wasn't in the best shape. She had osteoarthritis. Bad knees and hips. I told her it was because of all that kneeling and praying. We laughed about that." She gave a wistful smile.

"So she might have lost her balance on the steps in the bell tower?"

Mrs. Marberry nodded. "Certainly a possibility."

"Did she ever mention any conflicts with people at the church or school?"

"No, but I know something bothered her." She picked up her coffee mug and met my eyes. "Do you have a sister?"

"I have two of them—one older and one younger."

"So you know what I mean, then. You can tell with a sister when something isn't right."

As we sipped coffee, I told Anna Marberry about my sisters. *Establishing common ground puts the person at ease*, the chief had taught me. "My sister Stephanie, the oldest of us five kids, lives in The City. She dates a wealthy older man," I said.

Mrs. Marberry smiled. "Sounds like my husband. I understand the appeal."

I went on. "Other than family holidays, we rarely speak. She's busy with her life as an investment adviser. My younger sister Deanne is married and popping out babies—just had number four—in another city. She and I don't have much in common anymore either."

"Don't let your sisters drift away," Anna said with a sad shake of her head. "One day it will be too late."

Note to self: Call sisters to check in.

I asked, "So your sister gave you no clues as to what was bothering her?"

She shook her head. "No. When I pressed her, she said it was something from long ago. Nothing she could do anything about now."

"No other details. Names? Places? Dates?"

She shook her head. "Nothing specific. But she did say something odd one day. She said some sins can't be forgiven. That was such a peculiar thing for her to say because we're taught to confess and be forgiven. Simple as that."

A bell chimed somewhere in Hidden Valley. "Time for my yoga class." She stood, extending that soft hand.

I thanked her, expressed my condolences again, handed her my card with the usual "if you think of anything else" spiel, and left.

It was just after four when I stopped back at TriMak. Germany wasn't there. The place was locked up tight, and the lights were off. My stomach clenched while I looked around the office reception area for any sign of a struggle.

Snarky had some thoughts. *Duh. If Germany was kidnapped, would he turn the lights off and lock the doors before he left? You're brilliant, Sherlock.*

Nothing looked out of order. I sat at his desk and texted him.

Less than a minute later, he texted back:

> M fine went home early C U next wk

I reminded him I'd be at the convent. He shot back:

> HV FUN <angel emoji>

I sat at Germany's desk in the dark, opened the browser on my phone, and asked Google about sins and forgiveness. Google agreed with Mrs. Marberry. Christian theology holds that all sins are forgivable, except for "blasphemy against the Holy Spirit," whatever that meant. The "seven deadly sins"— pride, greed, lust, envy, gluttony, wrath, and sloth—were just part of the human condition. Could anyone say they were free of those? If those sent you to hell, it would be mighty crowded down there.

I decided to go home and ask the Supreme Authority—my grandmother—about the whole sin thing. I stood to leave and glanced out the TriMak front window at the street just in time to see the yellow Camaro roll past slowly as the driver stared into our window.

I hit the floor next to Germany's desk. Had he seen me? I hoped not. I lay there a couple of minutes, then crawled around the partition in front of the desk. I looked out at the street. No sign of the car.

I scooted to the back door, set the security alarm, locked up, ran to Cricket, and headed to Gram's. My heart racing, I kept an eye on the rearview mirror. Nobody followed me, as far as I could tell.

I sat in the car behind Gram's house until I felt calm. No sense rushing into the house and getting Gram upset.

She was in the kitchen putting the finishing touches on a pan of cheesy hash browns—one of my absolute favorite things Gram makes. A glazed ham sat in a pan on top of the stove.

I sat at the kitchen table, fiddling with the hen and rooster salt and pepper shakers. "Gram, are there any unforgivable sins?"

She shot me a look, frowning. "Why? What have you done?"

I laughed. "Nothing! I'm just asking from a philosophical point of view."

She shrugged. "I'm no expert. You should talk to Pastor Gunderson." The head honcho at Our Savior's Lutheran.

"Not that big a deal. I just want to know what *you* think," I said.

"Well, I don't think there is anything beyond God's forgiveness. Jesus paid it all, like the hymn says. Took all our sins to the cross."

I argued, "What about rape? Or hurting children? That must be unforgivable."

She shook her head. "Nope. I believe Jesus's sacrifice covers everything. Of course, we do need to repent and ask for forgiveness."

"No punishment for doing bad stuff? What's to keep people from just sinning all over the place and then saying, 'Oops, sorry. Forgive me.' That doesn't seem right."

"'Ask and ye shall be forgiven,' the Bible says. Period. And I don't question God's Word." She seemed so confident.

"Sounds a little too easy," I said.

"Sin has its own punishment. Think of how guilty you feel when you do wrong. That's the real suffering that our sin causes us. The guilt and shame."

She had a point. I'd certainly suffered for my stupid choices in the past.

But then again, I have a conscience.

CHAPTER ELEVEN

I F YOU'VE BEEN TO Three Rivers, you know this town goes a little crazy at Halloween time. Everyone decorates to the hilt—houses, yards, businesses—and there's the parade and the bonfire the Saturday before Halloween. And there are costume parties. Lots and lots of costume parties.

Nick invited me to one such party on Friday night. He was leaving on Saturday for a family trip celebrating his grandfather's ninetieth birthday and would be gone most of the following week.

The party was at the home of one of Nick's friends from high school—Brent "Spider" Spidowski. I recognized half the people there but hadn't hung out with them in school. Like Nick, they were the cool kids. Several of them seemed surprised to see me there with Nick, but I might have been imagining that.

Last Halloween, I dressed as Rosie the Riveter—a last-minute costume after my then-sort-of-boyfriend flaked out on me. He was going to be Captain Hook, but he dumped me, and he gave my Peter Pan costume to somebody else. This year, Nick and I decided to be Gomez and Morticia from the Addams family.

I was a divine Morticia. White makeup on my face, long black wig. Fake fingernails. My boobs looked good, jacked up in the low-cut, tight-fitting, floor-length black dress, slit on both sides almost to my behind, so I didn't have to walk with Morticia's little mincing steps. Yes, I'm proud to say I made one fine Morticia.

Nick made a comical Gomez. He looked silly with the thin mustache. He'd put something in his hair to blacken it, and he slicked it down. Ugliest striped suit ever with giant shoulders made of some kind of shiny polyester material—the kind of polyester you can cram into an empty mayonnaise jar, leave it for a year, and pull it out unwrinkled.

Nick called me "*Cara mia*" and kissed my hand a lot, asking me to speak French. So ooh-la-la. So Gomez.

Spider introduced me to his girlfriend, a girl named Hillary, who was dressed like a sexy Little Bo Peep, in a short, ruffly pink and white dress and a long blonde wig with ringlets. White thigh-high stockings and a shepherd's crook completed the look.

I didn't recognize her from high school, and when she said she'd graduated from Holy Assumption, that explained it. I went into detective mode. "I heard about that nun who died. Did you know her?"

"Yes, Sister Mary Agnes was my biology teacher. I liked her. She and my mother were friends. My mom went to Holy Assumption back when it was a college. She was in the last graduating class."

I'd already had a couple glasses—okay, maybe three—of wine, and I get stupid when I drink. That's why I asked, "Any reason you know of why anyone might have wanted Sister Mary Agnes dead?'

Anxious Me went ballistic. *OMG, OMG, shut up, shut up.*

Hillary frowned. "What?"

Stupid Me repeated the question.

She stepped back. "Why would you ask me that? What are you—a cop or something?"

How far should I take this? Tell her everything? I was tempted to whip out my business card and give her one of those looks and say something like, "Not a cop, no. I'm"—drum roll please—"Mack Prentice, Private Eye." I felt my cheeks redden under Morticia's makeup. I gave a weak laugh, did a hair flip, and tried a Morticia imitation. "Not a cop, darling. Just morbidly curious."

Hillary's look of disgust told me I was pathetic. She walked away, shaking her head.

I flashed back to my high school loser days, to that old rivalry between kids from public school versus private school. The feeling that the girls from Holy Assumption were prettier, smarter, and more desirable than we were. The private school girls came from richer families—they had to be to afford the tuition. Better clothes, better boyfriends, better futures.

I went into the bathroom, and Snarky sneered at me from the mirror. *Way to go, Sherlock. What is your problem? You're going undercover next week. Under. Cover. Don't be stupid. The chief will have your hide if you blow this.*

Anxious tried to defend me. *It's that old feeling of not good enough and wanting to impress her.*

Snarky: *Get your head out of your butt, or you're going to blow this case before you even get started.*

A couple of hours and a couple more glasses of wine later, the party started breaking up. Nick drove me home and, over decaf and a plate of Gram's brownies, we kissed.

Let's be honest. We were making out on the couch. The wine made my head fuzzy and my tongue thick. I whispered, "Nick, we can do it tonight if you want."

Real smooth, Snarky hissed.

Rational Me knew I'd just be using him to feel less like a loser, but the rest of me didn't care.

Just don't do it on the table, Anxious Me said.

Nick smiled at me. *Uh, those dimples!* "You know I want you, but I want to wait."

Snarky took over my mouth. "You want to 'wait'?" Snarky let fly. "Seriously? For what?" *Who waits these days?* "It's not like we're in high school and saving ourselves for The One."

"I'm not saying that. I just want to wait until the time is right for us, until we're serious." He blushed.

Adorable.

He finished off a brownie, washed it down with coffee, then said, "I mean serious, you know, like *committed*."

"Like exclusive?" Nick knew that I'd gone out with Vince. Vince knew that I'd gone out with Nick. Just a crazy gal playing the field—*c'est moi. Ooh, Tish, speak French to me, cara mia!* My head felt fuzzier, and my tongue thicker.

Nick's face looked a little blurry as I tried to tune in to his words. His lips looked very kissable as he said, "Well, yeah, exclusive, but more than just not dating other people."

"What's more than that? Engaged? Married?"

He gave a little lopsided smile, his right dimple deepening. He winked at me, I think. Nick drained his decaf and stood, reached for my hands, and helped me to my feet. The room gave a little spin as he took me in his arms and said, "What am I waiting for? It's you. *You* are worth waiting for."

He kissed me—a long, soft kiss that spoke volumes, and if I'd been sober, I might have been able to hear what the kiss was saying.

I leaned against the door jamb as I watched the taillights of Nick's Land Rover disappear around the corner. He was such a sweet guy, so caring, so polite. Had he said we should get married? That was all well and good for the future, but what about now? I needed somebody *now*.

Chloe gave a meow at my feet and wound herself around my calves. I picked her up as I shut the door. "What's wrong with me, girl?" I sat on the couch, Chloe on my lap. I repeated the question. "What's wrong with me?" Billy couldn't keep his hands off me in high school, but that's high school. Other guys seemed to find me attractive, or cute, or maybe funny, but I didn't seem to inspire the kind of animal passion other girls enjoyed.

Maybe being a just-right, Goldilocks kind of girl, as Gram describes me, leaves me on the "meh" side of romantic attraction. I asked the cat, "Am I just 'meh'? Maybe I should color my hair. Or wear more skirts, like my mother says. What do you think, Chloe?"

I started to carry her up to the loft, then remembered the roof issue. I'd have to sleep on the couch. I set Chloe down, went up the rest of the stairs, holding the handrail tightly. *Maybe Sister Mary Agnes was drunk that night.*

A wave of shame hit me. *Don't be so crass. The poor woman is dead.*

I grabbed my pajamas, my pillow, and the comforter from my bed and brought them to the couch. I went to the bathroom and cleaned Morticia off my face. The room gave a little spin as I looked at the girl in the mirror. "You are meh," I told her. "And admit it. You drink too much."

Meh Me had no response to that.

I flopped onto the couch, begging the room to hold still as I fell—hard—into sleep.

CHAPTER TWELVE

I WOKE SATURDAY MORNING FEELING like a flock of sheep had spent the night on my tongue. Sleeping on the couch had given me a stiff neck. I took a long, hot shower, letting the steaming water soothe my cramped muscles. I brushed my teeth extra-long and popped a couple of Excedrin with a tall glass of water. I checked the mirror. No trace of Morticia remained. Rational Me suggested again that maybe I was drinking too much. *Yeah, yeah, I know.*

I slipped into a pair of sweatpants, an oversized sweatshirt, soft socks, and my slippers, and I started to feel human again. I texted Nick.

> Sorry about last nite <sad face>

A couple seconds later, I got:

> No worries <zen face>

I remembered Little Bo Peep and called Nick. He answered, his voice warm and soft. "Good morning, gorgeous," he said. I pictured him in his bed. Next to me.

Lonely Me whispered, *We could wake up to that voice every day for the rest of our lives, right?*

I said, "Sorry again about being such a dope last night."

"Like I said—no worries. What's up?"

"I need to talk to Bo Peep."

He chuckled. "Okay . . . ?"

"That girl dressed like Bo Peep at the party. Spider's girl-friend. Hillary something. I need to talk with her. Can you get her number for me?"

A few minutes later, Nick—reliable, dependable Nick—texted the girl's full name and number. I called Hillary Sharp, apologized for freaking her out at the party. I explained that I was, actually, a licensed detective and that I wanted to speak with her mother about Sister Mary Agnes.

Bo Peep obliged, and a minute later, I was leaving her mother, Lillian Sharp, a voicemail, asking her to get back to me as soon as possible about Sister Mary Agnes's death.

It was almost ten-thirty. I headed to Gram's just as she was taking a pan of homemade cinnamon rolls from the oven.

I bent over the pan and took a big sniff. "Mmm. I could smell these all the way from the carriage house. Heaven better have cinnamon rolls, or I'm not going."

Gram started to remind me that in heaven, we won't care about cinnamon rolls. She stopped mid-sentence as my mother stomped in through the back door, slamming it shut.

I asked, "Something wrong, Mom?" *A brilliant detective picks up on subtle clues.*

She glared at me. "Obviously!"

Gram laid a hand on my mother's shoulder. "Sit down, dear. Have a cinnamon roll and a glass of milk. It'll make it all better."

My mother shot her a look. "I'm not a child! A cinnamon roll can't fix everything!"

Gram hugged her. "You'll always be *my* child. Now sit down and tell me what's going on."

My mother plopped onto a chair and covered her face with her hands. I sat across from her and waited in silence, as Gram piled cinnamon rolls on a plate before bringing that and three glasses of milk to the table. Gram and I ate our rolls and sipped milk as we waited.

A roll and a half later, my mother let out a sigh and looked up. "It's Duncan." My mother and Duncan had been dating for a year and had had spats off and on—usually because my mother was being anxious.

Gram said, "Oh dear. What's wrong with Duncan?"

"What's wrong with him is the stupid jerk is talking about getting married!" She said that as if marriage were the vilest thing anyone could do.

Gram smiled. "Why, that's wonderful, Barbara! You deserve to be happy!"

"Happy? You think I'm not happy now? I'm happy—delighted—to have things stay just the way they are! Marriage only leads to misery. I'm not going to let any man ruin my life—not again!"

She was referring, I knew, to my father. He left when I was little. Walked out one night to get cigarettes and never came back, leaving her with five kids to support. She took a giant wad of cinnamon roll, stuffed it into her mouth, and glugged half her glass of milk. She swallowed hard.

Gram said, "Marriage doesn't always bring misery, dear."

My mom sneered. "Oh really? What about yours? Your first husband died suddenly, just when you two were about to enjoy retirement. Your next husband was a cheater who died in the parking lot of the senior center humping some—"

"Now you just watch it there, girl!" Gram snapped, holding up a hand. "Chester might have been irresistible to the ladies, but if it weren't for him, I wouldn't have this house or the money." Thanks to Chester, Gram was "well fixed," as they say.

My mother glared at her. "Were you happy with him?"

Gram nodded. "Happy enough."

My mother rolled her eyes. "And now what? Are you happy playing nursemaid to Nathan? When do you get a break?"

I held my breath as Gram gave my mother a pitying look. "God knows what we can handle, Barbara. God supplies the strength we need for whatever comes our way. I trust the good Lord every day."

"But are you *happy*?"

Gram gave a soft smile. "You young people talk as if being 'happy' is the end-all, be-all in life. Happiness comes and goes. Nobody is happy all the time. That's not how life works. You take the bad with the good. That's just how it is."

My mother leaned back in her chair. "Well, I've had enough bad to last my lifetime, and I'm not about to give up the good I have right now."

Gram said, "Duncan is good for you, isn't he?"

My mom took another angry bite of a cinnamon roll. "I thought so until he started talking about marriage. Stupid jerk!" She took a bigger bite and said as she chewed, "What's wrong with staying the way we are?"

I asked, "Did you ask him that?"

My mother nodded and swallowed.

Gram asked, "And what did he say?"

We waited as she washed the roll down with milk. She took a paper napkin from Gram's chicken-shaped napkin holder and wiped her mouth. She finished her milk and wiped her mouth again.

This was getting ridiculous. I said, "C'mon, Mom! What did Duncan say?"

Her cheeks turned pink, and she wrinkled her nose. Her voice got soft. "The stupid jerk said that he wanted my face to be the first thing he saw in the morning. Every morning. For the rest of his life."

Gram and I looked at each other with the look you have at the end of a good rom-com, when the boy finally gets the girl. I said, "Aww . . ."

My mom scowled at us. "You two are so sappy! How can I trust him? Men say things like that. They say whatever they think you need to hear so you'll—you know."

Gram and I exchanged another look, disbelief or something this time. Gram said, "He said that so you'll what? Sleep with him? A little late for that, don't you think?"

My mother looked at Gram and blushed, crimson this time. "You know what I mean!"

How old do you have to be to stop being embarrassed to talk about sex in front of your mother? Older than my mother, evidently.

Gram chuckled. "So he's been getting the milk for free, and he still wants to buy the cow. How about that!"

"For God's sake, I'm not a cow!" My mother took her plate and glass to the sink, then came back to the table, leaning on her palms as she looked at us, tears rimming her lower lids.

"Seriously. I want to know. How can I trust him? How can I trust any man?"

I said nothing. Every man I ever loved had left me. I knew from doing therapy in the past with Dr. Angela that I had some serious daddy-abandonment issues of my own. I shifted in my chair so I, too, was facing Gram. "Yeah, Gram, how can we trust any man?"

Gram gave us a little head shake. "Well, we certainly can't trust them all. We know that would be foolish. We take them on a case-by-case basis." Gram reached across the table to grasp both my mother's hands. "Barbara, Duncan is a good man, and he's offering you his heart, a home, a future. Please promise me you'll think about it."

My mother blinked back tears, then gave a quick nod. "Yeah. Fine. Whatever." With that, she headed upstairs.

"Wow," I said. "This is big, Gram."

She nodded. "Yep. Huge."

Half an hour later, I went to my mother's bedroom on the second floor of the Victorian. I rapped lightly, then poked my head around the half-open door. "Permission to enter, your majesty?"

My mom chuckled. "You may enter."

I sat on the edge of the bed. "So tell me, Mom. Did Duncan actually propose?" I wanted to get the skinny on this, just in case Nick or Vince decided to give me an official proposal. "Maybe he's just talking about moving in together? You spend enough time there as it is. You might as well be living together."

"I don't think that's what he meant. He's got some old-fashioned notions."

"But he didn't actually propose."

"Well, not in so many words. It was that thing about wanting to see my face. I heard that, and I bolted."

"I get that—the bolting part. Because my dad left, and Papa Powell died, and Chester cheated, and Billy cheated—" I stopped. My mother looked bemused. "What? What are you smiling at?"

She gave a throaty chuckle. "You realize you are making my case, right? Men break our hearts. They lie, they cheat, they die. Or like Gram, they end up needing us to take care of them. Look around, Mackenzie. Men make us miserable. Simple as that."

"So you're miserable with Duncan?"

She shook her head. "Not yet. We'll be fine if he just stops the nonsense about getting married or even living together. I like the status quo. It works fine for us."

"Maybe for you, but maybe not for him."

"He's not the only guy around. If he doesn't like it, there are other fish—" She stopped. "Oh, good grief, what am I saying? I don't want to start dating again. I've looked at those online sites, and there's nothing out there. Mucho Matches? Mucho Losers is what they really mean."

"You're right, Mom. Plenty of nothing out there." I'd toyed with online dating myself and found nobody worth my time. I thought about Heather and this new guy she'd met. Maybe he'd be an exception.

My mother said, "Easy for you to say since I believe you have two men interested in you."

I smiled, picturing Vince and then Nick. Both adorable. Both desirable. *Really, really desirable*, Lonely Me whispered. I got lost in thought about both of their, um, respective desirableness, until my mother cleared her throat.

"Ahem! Mackenzie, we're talking about me, remember?"

"Oh, right. Sorry, Mom. So the big question is—and I don't remember where I heard this—are you better off with him or without him?"

"Dear Abby always asks that."

I looked at my mom. "So are you better off with Duncan or without him?"

She gave a shrug. "That's what I have to figure out. Right now, it's a toss-up."

"I'll leave you to it then." I closed her door and went back downstairs. I said goodbye to Gram and Nathan, who were in the family room watching *Little House on the Prairie*.

As I walked to the carriage house, the question rang. *Better off with Nick or Vince? With either? Or neither? Better off single?*

CHAPTER THIRTEEN

B ACK IN THE CARRIAGE house, I took two more Excedrin, poured a tall glass of sparkling water, and brought it to the couch. Chloe jumped onto my lap, curled up, and purred.

I thought about my ex, Billy. We'd met in high school. Just kids. Married in our early twenties, never expecting the troubles we had. Too much drinking on both our parts. Too much cheating on his part.

I said aloud to the cat, "*Any* cheating is too much, isn't it, girl?" She purred louder. Are cats monogamous? Or are we the only mammals tormented by the expectation of fidelity?

We don't go into marriage expecting trouble. We go in expecting the fairytale happily ever after, don't we? I was sure that when Gram married Nathan a decade ago, she didn't expect to be taking care of him. Or did she? Is there an age where we just assume one of us will end up taking care of the other? Gram says caring for others is the blessing and burden of life.

My mother was looking at marriage as all burden. No doubt her anxiety was clouding her thinking. Probably that old fear of abandonment thing. I have that fear too.

Was fear the reason I waffled between Vince and Nick? Afraid to choose safe and predictable Nick because life with him might get boring? Afraid to choose Vince because he was wild and dangerous, and I knew his first marriage had ended because of cheating. Vince said his wife had cheated first. Did that matter? Could I trust him a hundred percent?

Chloe shifted her body. "Am I crazy, girl? Should I call Doctor Angela? Get some therapy?" I picked her up by her armpits and held her in front of me. "What do you think? Am I crazy?"

Chloe looked at me and let out a meow, twisted herself out of my grip, and ran upstairs to the loft. I hollered after her. "Sure! Run away from the crazy person!"

I looked in my phone contacts. Yep, there was Dr. Angela's number. I stopped short of actually leaving her a voicemail. I finished my water and tidied the kitchen. It was almost noon. Halloween parade time.

I found Gram and Nathan in their usual parade-watching spot, in lawn chairs in front of Lou's Vintage. I sat on the curb in front of Gram. Most years, I attend the parade in costume, but I'd been Morticia last night with Nick, and tonight I'd be in that costume again when I went out with Vince. It felt good to take a little break and just be regular old me.

Midway through the parade, a float with a cardboard haunted house came by. Students from Holy Assumption atop the float were made up like zombies. Other students in various costumes walked alongside the float, handing out candy and invitations to the Holy Assumption school carnival on Halloween.

I ducked my head so the kids wouldn't see me. Why? Because I'd be at the school on Monday, and I didn't want anyone to be able to say, "Hey, I saw you at the parade, and you weren't wearing your nun outfit. What's the deal?" Which was ridiculous because teenagers pay no attention to adults, in public or at home. I remember. The last thing teenage me cared about was what adults were doing. We're in our own world at that age, aren't we? And that's the way it is supposed to be. As I recall, I spent a lot of time rolling my eyes and saying, "Whatever" to my mother.

As the kids from Holy Assumption passed by, Gram tapped me on the shoulder. "Look, Mackenzie. Those are your future students."

I ducked my head farther away from the parade. "Be quiet, Gram. I told you I'll be undercover. I don't need anyone noticing me here today."

Gram leaned closer and whispered, "Gotcha! Your secret is safe."

If only that were true.

As the Holy Assumption kids moved on down the street, Lou Burgess came to sit with us. Her vintage store provides endless options for costumes, and today she was dressed as Elton John. She wore a purple-and-pink print blazer, wild hot pink pants, huge square-rimmed glasses, and a thick blonde wig.

I turned to her. "Hey, Elton—"

She held up a hand, "Sir Elton, if you please."

I laughed. "Okay, Sir Elton. You got my message?"

Elton nodded, and the big glasses slid down Lou's nose. She shoved them back into place.

I said, "I'm working a case that will take all my time."

"Ooh, what's it about?"

I shook my head. "Can't say, and I'd appreciate it if you didn't press for details."

Lou nodded, holding the glasses in place with an index finger. "No problem."

I turned back toward the parade, hoping Gram would honor our pinky-swear and keep her mouth shut with her buddy Lou.

The parade ended with the street sweeper rolling by. I left to meet Tansy and Jade at Tres Hermanos, the best Mexican restaurant in this part of the state. The interior is painted red and yellow, with cactus motifs. Little lights strung from the ceiling are chili-pepper shaped, and the restrooms are marked "Hombres" and "Mujeres."

We waited for one of their cushy booths to open and settled in. Jade and Tansy sat together on one side, and I took the other. Our waiter, Steve, according to his name tag, brought us a basket of warm tortilla chips and three types of salsa for dipping. Hot, hotter, and hottest.

Jade picked up a chip and shook salt on it before dipping it into the hottest. She took a bite. Sweat formed on her upper lip. "Mmm! Muy caliente!"

Tansy followed suit, taking a bigger chip and more of the hottest salsa. She took a bite. Then she teared up and started to cough. She grabbed for her water.

Jade stopped her. "No! Water makes it worse. Eat more chips!"

Tansy's coughing and tears finally stopped, and she blew her nose. "Lesson learned," she said, her voice hoarse.

I munched plain chips as we discussed menu options. I decided on the chimichanga with ground beef, beans, and rice. Jade and Tansy decided to share a sizzling platter of fajitas. We ordered a double side of guacamole and extra sour cream.

We'd taken our first bites, and I said, "Nick wants to wait."

They exchanged a look. Tansy asked, "Wait for what?"

"For sex."

Jade gave me wide eyes. "What? You mean you two haven't done it yet?"

I shook my head. "He wants to wait until we're serious, or committed, or something," I said as I scooped a heaping spoonful of guac onto my chimichanga.

Jade looked shocked. "What? Who does that anymore?"

Tansy shrugged. "I don't know. I think it's kind of sweet."

I looked at them. "Would either of you wait?"

Jade laughed. "Well, since I don't care if I ever get married, I don't know what I'd be waiting for."

I turned to Tansy. "How about you, Tans? Are you a waiting kind of gal?"

She shook her head. "You gotta ride that horse before you invite him into the stable."

We all laughed. Jade said, "You take a car for a test drive before you put your money down, right? And you're only gonna have the car for a few years, not stuck with it for the rest of your life. I don't want to be 'stuck' with anyone for life unless I'm sure he—or she—is worth it." Jade has a flexible approach to romance.

Tansy said, "You don't buy clothes before you try them on. You check out a house before you commit to a mortgage. I don't get why a physical relationship—like a really, *really* important part of life—is left to chance."

Jade said, "Yeah, what if he's just really bad in bed?"

Tansy said, "You need to have all the information before you can make an informed decision."

Jade waved a hand. "Why even get married at all? Just go with the flow. No strings. No drama, no trauma."

This reminded me of the conversations we had back in school when we were just learning about all these things. How long to wait, how far to go, how far was "too far." I wondered what kind of conversations Sister Mary Agnes had with her students. "Waiting until marriage" was certainly the rule, wasn't it? Abstinence was the party line, right? My stomach tightened, worrying about questions they might have for me. What would I say?

I came back to the present when Tansy said, "I get it, Mack. Nick is a real sweetie. If you don't want him, I wouldn't mind taking him for a test drive."

I hadn't really thought about other women wanting Nick. I don't know why I hadn't thought about that, but there it was. The possibility of losing Nick, having his attention shift to someone else. I felt a pang deep in my chest. Maybe I loved the guy. Could that be it?

Jade said, "Not me. I like a little spice. Nick is just a little too . . ." She looked at the ceiling, searching for the right word. "Vanilla. Yeah, that's it. He's vanilla. Like pudding. Bland. Not real exciting."

I had to speak up. "He is *not* vanilla. He's reliable. Predictable. Dependable."

Tansy joined in defending Nick. "Yeah, that's important in a guy. Who needs all that drama that other guys bring? Wondering if he's gonna call. Wondering what he's thinking."

I smiled. "Nick's not afraid to share a feeling."

Jade said, "If a guy wants to share his feelings, he can go share them all over somebody else. I'll take a Vince over a Nick any day."

Tansy said, "Mmm, yeah. That Vince Hampton is one magnificent specimen of manhood." She closed her eyes and said it again. "Mmm, yeah. Magnificent."

"Hey!" I gave her a little slap on the arm. "Quit drooling over my Vince."

Tansy laughed. "*Your* Vince? *Your* Nick? You don't seem to really want either one of them."

I huffed. "What makes you say that? I actually want both of them!"

Jade said, "Doesn't look like it to me, girl. You're playing with both of them, and if you keep doing that, you'll lose them both."

Tansy nodded. "Jade's right. You need to decide, Mack, before they both go away."

Decide? How? I voiced the question. "How am I supposed to do that?"

Jade said, "Flip a coin."

I shook my head. "Deciding who you might spend the rest of your life with requires more than a coin toss."

Tansy said, "Okay, so do a pros and cons chart. That'll help you see if there are any deal breakers."

I nodded. "That sounds like a mature, reasonable approach."

Jade scoffed. "And clinical. And boring. Mack, it comes down to a simple question: Which one of those guys makes you hot? Which one would you like to wake up with every morning?"

I said, "Vince scores pretty high on the hotness scale." They both nodded vigorously as I continued. "But I could wake up to Nick's sweet face every morning. And he'd make me pancakes."

"Probably shaped like Mickey Mouse," Tansy said. We all laughed.

Jade said, "And Vince would roll over, slap you on the behind and say, 'Woman! Make food!'"

I shook my head. "You guys think of them that way? Like Nick is some little boy, and Vince is a caveman?"

They looked at each other and then turned to me and said, in unison, "Yes."

I finished the last of my platter, swung my legs out of the booth, and stood. "Well, you obviously don't know them at all." I put cash on the table for the bill. "I have to get going."

They each pulled out cash, added it to mine, and got out of the booth. Jade said, "You're not mad, are you?" I assured her I wasn't.

Tansy said, "We were just teasing. They're both great guys."

I said, "Yeah, that's the problem. They're both great.

"Nice problem to have, though," Tansy said.

I couldn't argue with that.

CHAPTER FOURTEEN

B ACK AT THE CARRIAGE house, I took a nap, then put my
Morticia face and costume back on. It was 8:30 when Vince
showed up. Tricorn hat, leather pants, and vest. Shirt open to
reveal his muscled chest. With his swarthy, dark looks, he made
a great pirate.

"Jack Sparrow, madam," he said, removing his hat and
sweeping forward into a low bow. He came back up, shook
his head to move the long braids and beads of his wig, then
replaced the hat. "Cool, huh?"

*What's with me and pirates? Last year, Captain Hook. This
year, Jack Sparrow.*

As we walked out to Vince's truck holding hands, I decided
that Jack Sparrow and Morticia made a fine couple.

Old Town Tap was jumpin' when we got there. They have a
Halloween deal every year—first drink is free if you show up in
costume. I started with a Long Island iced tea. And then Vince
bought me another.

The ceiling was draped with orange and white twinkle lights. The music was great, and Vince is a good dancer. He is an exceptionally good slow dancer. My arms around his neck, resting my head on his shoulder, I felt sort of melty. I didn't remember him smelling this good. His arms were so strong, his hands so hot against the small of my back.

We danced. We laughed. We kissed on the dance floor. We danced some more. We drank some more. We kissed in a booth. Then kissed some more.

I get stupid when I drink. Two Long Islands are plenty. So I had a third.

Vince said he was fine to drive me home, and I believed him. The drive back to my place seemed longer than usual, but booze distorts your judgment of time and space.

Vince had insisted we eat from the free buffet Old Town Tap offered. While we drove, I finished off the barbecued chicken wings we brought from the bar. We made it to the carriage house. He supported me as we went inside.

I kissed Vince again. Not one of those gentle kisses. I grabbed him by the front of his pirate shirt and gave him a full-on smacker. I tried my sexiest pose, adjusting my Morticia wig with one hand and the other hand on my hip. "Wanna go upstairs?" I asked, then remembered that the loft was unusable until the roof got fixed. "No, wait. We can do it right here on the couch." I backed up to the dining table. "Or right here?" I leaned over the table, extending an arm as if I was going to sweep everything off it onto the floor, just like you see in the movies.

I moved toward him, getting so close that he leaned away. "How about it, Jack Sparrow?" That came out "Sh-parrow" along with a little blob of spit that landed on his shirt. As he wiped that off, I went in for another kiss. He leaned farther away.

Like I said, I get stupid when I drink. I can't imagine how Vince had the presence of mind—not like him at all—to resist all my gorgeousness, but he grabbed my upper arms and held me at arm's length. "No thanks," he said.

I scowled at him as I stifled a belch. "*No thanks?* A girl makes you an offer like that, and you say 'no thanks'? You've been after me for months, and now you say no? What the—?"

He laughed. *Laughed!* "Don't get all insulted. I just mean no thanks for tonight." His eyes drilled into mine. "*Just* for tonight. Understand? I want you to be *sober* when we do that." He slowed, parsing out every syllable. "I want your *full* attention. I want you *one-hundred-percent present* when we do that. Do you understand?"

A tingle ran through me. I felt like I was collapsing into those dark eyes. Intoxicating, the smell of whatever it was he was wearing—like leather, smoke, and bourbon. So intense, his energy. So compelling, his voice, rumbling deep. I felt dizzy. Maybe it was Vince. Or maybe it was the booze.

He walked me back to the couch. "You get some sleep, okay?" He laid me onto the cushions, put a throw pillow under my head, and, ever-so-gently, covered me with the granny-square afghan Gram had given me as a carriage-house-warming present.

He patted the afghan as he smiled down at me. "Sleep now."

I lay there as Vince left, the door clicking closed behind him.

Chloe walked to the couch and purred up at me. I sat up. My stomach churned. She jumped up and sat next to me, cocking her head as if to say, *What the hell?*

I laid a hand on her head. The room did a little spin. *How did I get so drunk?*

I spoke aloud, slurring my words. "Dude's been after me forever, and now I give him the chance, and he leaves? Who does that? What man in his right mind says no to that?"

Chloe had no answer. I got up and stumbled to the bathroom, grumbling to myself. "Jack Sparrow. Jack*ass* is more like it. Wants me to be *sober* when we do it. What*ever*!" I checked the mirror. Morticia's wig was crooked. The white makeup had smeared off on the right side, probably onto that pillow on my couch. Two of my fake nails had popped off. There was barbecue sauce on my chin from the wings we'd brought home from the Tap.

Chloe rubbed against the back of my calves. I pointed at my reflection. "Seriously, Chloe. What man could resist all this?"

Cats can laugh. I swear, cats can laugh.

I changed out of the costume into the pajamas I'd hung on the back of the bathroom door and wiped most of Morticia off my face. In the kitchen, I took two aspirins with half a glass of water with baking soda—a hangover prevention trick I'd learned somewhere along my drinking journey. Maybe Billy taught me that. *Aw, Billy. Sorry it didn't work out for us. And now you're gone. Forever.*

Feeling melancholy—*Sappy drunk*, Snarky whispered—I brought another glass of water to the couch and sat. Alone. Two guys in my life. Neither one wanted me. Both wanted to wait, they said. *How long?* Lonely Me wondered.

I closed my eyes and lay down. The room started spinning. I shifted positions. More spinning. I sat up. My stomach lurched. I just made it to the bathroom before I lost it.

Ten minutes later, I lay curled on the tile floor. The bathroom held still.

Badass was royally ticked. *What the hell, Vince? Reject me? Loser!*

Anxious had another take on the whole situation. Neither Vince nor Nick nor any other man would ever want me. *We are not "just right." Not pretty enough, or cool enough, or whatever enough to ever, ever, EVER have another man in our life. Meh! Meh! Meh!*

I slept on the bathroom floor until after three, when I crawled to the couch and passed out again.

CHAPTER FIFTEEN

SOMETIMES YOU WAKE UP bright-eyed and bushy-tailed, Gram says. Not today. A litter of puppies had spent the night in my mouth. The sun brightened my living room. I opened one eye. Nine-fifteen. I groaned. My head throbbed; my stomach felt queasy. I sat up, and everything felt worse. I made it to the bathroom, leaned my hands against the sink, and bent toward the mirror, squinting.

Vestiges of Morticia's white makeup stuck to the edges of my face. Thick black eyeliner had melted onto my cheeks. My hair had some serious bedhead—or more accurately, couch head—going on. A dried smear of red on my chin was barbecue sauce.

Gram would say I looked "a fright." She would not be wrong about that.

I squished my eyes closed, replaying the scene with Vince. Rational Me looked in the mirror. *Things always seem worse than they actually were. Don't beat yourself up. I'm sure Vince isn't worrying about it.*

Snarky laughed. *Yeah, right. He's probably already told all his fire station buddies, including Greg, how stupid you are.* I groaned again. I hadn't thought about that.

Rational stepped in. *He's not some adolescent. He's a decent guy.*

I took a deep breath and got into the shower with that thought on repeat. *He's a decent guy. Don't worry about it.*

I felt more human after the shower and some Excedrin. I couldn't imagine how much worse I would have felt without the purge last night. I made some toast, buttered it, and sprinkled cinnamon and sugar on it. Made a half pot of coffee, poured a cup, and added a generous glug of heavy whipping cream.

At my dining table, I sipped coffee and planned my day. I'd be heading to the convent this afternoon and might be gone the whole week. I needed to clean my place before I left. I hate coming home to a mess.

The bathroom was a disaster. I cleaned with a barrage of the usual post-drunk regrets. The barrage starts with "why?" *Why did I drink so much last night? Why can't I just stop after a couple, like normal people do. Why indeed?*

Dr. Angela would say that there are people who can stop after a couple drinks. They don't have a problem. Then there are those of us who cannot stop, who drink to the point of stupid, or worse.

I'd like to think I'm in the former group, but experience tells me I'm not.

Anxious had thoughts of remorse and shame. *Oh God, what did you do? Made a complete fool of yourself, that's what you did!*

Rational Me stepped in. *You had to apologize to Nick. Now apologize to Vince. Perhaps in the future, you won't be so stupid, and there will be no need for morning-after apologies.*

Snarky hissed, *Fat chance!*

I called Vince, hoping I'd get his voicemail, but he picked up after four rings. "Hey, Mack. What's up?"

"Just calling to apologize for being so stupid last night."

"Don't sweat it. We all get that way sometimes. But I meant what I said. I do want you, but I want you sober." This was a fine thing coming from Vince, who on several occasions had drunk-texted me, sloppily, sappily.

"Well, I'm sorry. I shouldn't have had so much to drink."

"How about tonight? You busy? We could get dinner and then, who knows?"

Snarky said, *Ooh, he wants to strike while the iron is hot.*

Anxious: *Not ready for sober Vince, not after last night.* I said, "Sorry. I'll be at the convent."

A pause, then he laughed. "The convent? Last night wasn't *that* bad!"

I laughed too. It felt good to lighten things up. "I'm not *joining* the convent. It's just a work thing. Can't really talk about it, but I'll probably be there the rest of the week."

"Okay then. Maybe next weekend we can do something."

"Sure. Maybe. Sorry again about last night."

"We're good," he said, and we ended the call.

I felt relief. I'd made my amends to Vince. And I'd apologized to Nick. Rational Me said, *See? We don't need AA. We know how to make amends. But maybe we should try not drinking for a while.*

My cop-friend Heather had gotten sober with the help of AA. And certainly, when Billy and I were married, our drinking caused lots of drama. After we divorced, I went to one AA meeting as Doctor Angela suggested. I decided I wasn't like those people—they had *real* problems. I didn't have a *real* problem with drinking—I just drank too much sometimes.

Lately, I drank less often, but when I did, I couldn't seem to stop. And I was getting tired of hangovers. Heather had said something to me a while back about being glad to be sober, and how she stopped drinking "just in time."

Anxious Me whispered, *Maybe you should stop now, before something awful happens.* I knew the "something awfuls" she meant—drunk driving, causing an accident, ending up in jail.

I ignored them all and finished cleaning the kitchen, with a rising determination to stop drinking altogether.

A girl who can rescue others should be able to save herself. Right? Right!

CHAPTER SIXTEEN

G RAM'S DINING ROOM TABLE is usually crowded on Sundays after church. Family. Friends. People my grandmother invites on the way out of church. All are welcome.

Today was unusually quiet, which was fine with me since my head had a dull throb. *Two nights of drinking, you pay the price.* No arguing with Rational about that.

Gram, Nathan, and I enjoyed roast beef, mashed potatoes, gravy, buttermilk biscuits, and butter. Green beans. North country soul food, satisfying after a night of drinking, especially topped off with a glass of cold milk with chocolate cake for dessert.

I leaned back in the dining room chair, gave a sigh, and closed my eyes.

"Did you get enough to eat, dear?" Gram asked. That might have been sarcasm from someone who'd just witnessed the carnage as I devoured my dinner. But my sweet grandmother doesn't have a sarcastic bone in her body.

I nodded, eyes closed. "Plenty, Gram, as always."

"That's good. I don't want you to go into your investigation hungry."

I opened my eyes, raised an index finger to my lips. "That's top secret, Gram, remember?"

She did her lip-locking again, nodding.

I helped Gram clean up and then went back to the carriage house, went to my bedroom closet, and grabbed the suitcase I call my Bug Out Bag, aka "BOB." This is the suitcase my anxious mother encourages me to have in my car, especially in the winter, "just in case" I get stranded in a blizzard and have to stay overnight in a motel.

I opened Bob and checked my always-packed essentials. Toothbrush and paste, of course. Hairbrush and comb. A travel bottle of shampoo I'd picked up on my last stay at a motel. (The kind I always take and never use.) Bob held spare underwear. And deodorant, naturally.

I packed my TriMak flashlight—a heavy-duty police grade that the chief insisted we all have. He calls his "The Great Persuader."

What else would I need? I tried to imagine myself dressed as a nun. I pictured the stereotypical catholic girl in knee socks and plaid skirt. Did the kids at Holy Assumption wear uniforms? I grabbed my laptop and pulled up the school's website. No uniforms. Conservative clothing. No denim. No wearing what looks like underwear to school. How refreshing.

The website had a Bible quote:

> Do you not know that your body is a temple of the Holy Spirit within you, whom you have from God, and that you are not your own? For you have been

purchased at a price. Therefore, glorify God
in your body. —1 Corinthians 6:19–20

Below that, a photo showed a nun in conversation with a
couple of students. She wore a skirt and blouse with a short
veil on her head. A skirt meant pantyhose. I had none. I'd have
to swing by Target on the way to the convent. I dug a pair of
black loafers—my dress shoes—out of the back of the closet
and tossed them into Bob.

I looked around the bedroom. Anything else I might
need? Pajamas, of course. Since I didn't know what might
call me to action in the middle of the night, I packed a pair
of black sweatpants and a couple of tee shirts as well as a
heavy black sweatshirt. I was careful to avoid my TriMak shirts
and anything with logos.

I put Bob into Cricket and headed to Gram's to tell her
I was leaving. When I told her I needed pantyhose, she went
upstairs and came back with two pair, still in the little boxes.
Then she reached under her dress and stripped off the pair she
was wearing, rolled them up, and handed the ball to me. "These
are clean. Just wore them to church this morning," she said.

The ball of nylon was warm in my hand. Gram will give
you the shirt off her back, or the pantyhose off her legs, if you
need them.

CHAPTER SEVENTEEN

L ILLIAN SHARP CALLED ME back and agreed to meet with me before I headed to the convent. The Sharps live on the Hill, the ritzy section of Three Rivers where everybody who is anybody lives. (Since my family doesn't live there, I guess we all qualify as somebodies who are nobodies.)

She welcomed me so cordially, she must have thought I was somebody. We sat in the living room, sun streaming across the beige carpet. I'm always amazed at people who can keep beige carpeting clean in their homes. I can imagine how ours would have looked after us five kids had our way with it.

Mrs. Sharp sat back on the sofa. "I've known Sister Mary Agnes since I was in college at Holy Assumption. She'd just started teaching there. She'd come from another college out east somewhere, as I recall. I volunteered to help her with a project, and we became friends. I can't believe she's gone now. She was a mentor to me and such a dear friend." Mrs. Sharp looked out the living room window, gave a sigh, and turned back to me. "So what do you want to know? How can I help?"

"It is imperative that our conversation remain confidential, just between us. Agreed?"

She paused, considering, then nodded. "With Mary Agnes gone, I'm not really in touch with anyone at the convent. My daughter told me you're an investigator working undercover. Is that right?"

I nodded.

"How exciting," she said. "But I can't imagine the need for an investigation. Mary Agnes fell down the stairs. That's my understanding."

"I'm not sure there is anything more to the story. At this point, I'm just looking for general information. Can you tell me what it was like when you were in school there?"

She settled back against the couch and smiled. "Oh, my goodness, so many good memories of those days."

She talked for the next twenty minutes about all the fun she had, her classes. "My roommate and I were both art history majors. That was the fallback for a lot of girls. It gives you nothing but a college degree, but our real goal in life was to get our M.R.S. degree."

"I get it. Married."

She laughed. "Yes, that was the goal. And Holy Assumption had regular mixers with Ignatius, hoping to help us girls meet nice Catholic boys." I knew that Ignatius, an hour south of Three Rivers, was a men's college back then.

Her expression grew solemn. She looked down at her hands, fidgeting with her wedding rings. "Let me just start by saying we were 'good girls.' We went to church, followed the rules. My roommate had been seeing someone. She wouldn't tell me who it was, but I assumed it was a boy from Three Rivers. 'Townies,' we called them. Anyway, she got pregnant, then lost the baby. She couldn't tell her parents. They'd have disowned her, she said, and I have no doubt of that."

Mrs. Sharp met my eyes. "I'm the only one who even knew she'd been pregnant. I don't think the boy even knew. I promised her I'd keep her secret, and I have, all these years."

"That whole situation had to have been so difficult," I said.

"We girls didn't have a lot of options back then, you know. It wasn't like it is nowadays, with girls having babies and everybody being okay with it. Back then, 'unwed mothers' were sent away. The family might make up a story, like 'she's in Europe for the summer.' But we all knew what was really going on." She sighed. "It was so different back then. Now girls have the baby, keep it, live with the father, or not. It's a whole different world. Better, I think. More accepting. My husband would disagree with me, I know."

"Hillary's father was strict?"

"Oh, yes, definitely. No sex until marriage, and God help you if you stray from that. We met later in life. I was almost forty when I had Hillary. We didn't think we'd ever have children, and then, just when I thought that part of my life was over, surprise. She's our one and only, and my husband is incredibly protective of her."

I pictured Hillary in her Little Bo Peep getup at Spider's party. *What would Daddy think of that?* None of my business.

I steered our conversation back down memory lane. "Anything else you'd like to share?"

"Back at Holy Assumption, girls would sneak out of the dorm at night. I never did it, of course—I never even dated anyone until I met my husband. I was almost thirty by then." She paused.

I prompted her back to the story. "How could the girls sneak out without getting caught?" As if I didn't know how kids figure things out.

"There were these tunnels in the basement, and at the end of one of them was this ladder above a cistern. Up the ladder, through the hatch at the top, and freedom!" She laughed. "You had to stretch over the water to grab the ladder. One of the girls lost her footing and fell into the water. She came back to the dorm soaked. Lucky she didn't drown. Or worse, get caught by the nuns."

We chuckled over that, and she continued. "Usually, the girl would tell her boyfriend to wait for her by the hatch. Saturday nights, especially. There was probably a whole crowd of townies waiting by that hatch."

"Nobody ever got caught?"

"The nuns were oblivious, I guess, all tucked in at the convent for the night." She shook her head. "There was one night, I remember now, that one of the girls—Cheryl Spencer was her name—isn't it funny how you remember details like that? Anyway, I remember her coming back and telling me that the school custodian was waiting at the hatch when she pushed it open. He told her to never use the ladder again and to warn the rest of us to stop using it. He said it was too dangerous. I wonder now if he meant the danger of falling into the cistern or getting caught by the sisters. Especially Mary Agnes. She worried so about all of us."

"Did the girls stop?"

"The next person who tried reported back that the hatch had been sealed shut. That was that. Girls had to find other ways to sneak out, I guess. I never did. My parents would have skinned me alive if I tried anything."

We spent the next few minutes remembering the "good old days" when parents kept their children under control. I felt like an old, cranky person complaining about "kids these days."

"Are you still in touch with your college friends?" Perhaps one of them would have more information about Sister Mary Agnes.

"A few, very casually. Christmas cards, things like that."

"What about your roommate?"

Lillian pressed her lips together. "She died. She overdosed. We were all just shocked." She closed her eyes and lowered her head. She might have been praying. I waited. When she opened her eyes, she looked relieved. "I've held onto it long enough. I'm glad I was able to tell you."

She was out of stories, and I was out of time. I had to get to the convent. I gave her my card and asked her to call or text if she thought of anything else.

She met my eyes. "I've prayed for Mary Agnes so often. I hate to think she came to her moment of death in fear or pain."

"She's in a better place now." *What a nunny thing to say.* Snarky couldn't help herself.

Lillian Sharp smiled and nodded. "Indeed, yes, indeed."

CHAPTER EIGHTEEN

A S I DROVE AWAY from the Hill, I texted the chief to let him know I was heading to Holy Assumption. I parked Cricket at the corner of Harlow and Vine to look at my temporary new home. Built in the mid-1800s, Holy Assumption Church is an imposing red granite building in the Neo-Romanesque style, according to my online research. There's a large round stained-glass window above the front entrance and arched openings throughout. Broad concrete steps lead to the double doors, on either side of an imposing statue of Jesus, with arms open wide to welcome parishioners.

I looked up at the bell tower—three stories tall with large openings beneath a spire at the top. Where Sister Mary Agnes spent her last moments.

The convent, built at the same time and of the same red granite as the church, stands to the left. A large house with two stories and an attic, the convent has a front porch. Flowerpots along the path to the front door burst with bright yellow and orange chrysanthemums. Several flower boxes along the porch rail held the remains of summer flowers.

Neatly trimmed, low-growing junipers partially concealed the convent's crumbling foundation. The chief had mentioned that the parish needed funds. A sagging gutter above the second floor and a window with a crack covered with packing tape spoke to that need.

I said aloud, "Here's home for the next week, Jimbo. Impressive, isn't it?"

Jimbo gave a chirp. Happy or sad? No telling with a cricket.

To the right of the church stands the two-story school building, formerly Holy Assumption College for women, now Holy Assumption High School. According to my research, the college was built in the 1930s and was converted to a high school in the late 1960s.

Today, Holy Assumption High has a reputation for excellence in education, strict standards, a 99 percent graduation rate, and 85 percent of those graduates go on to further schooling. Some of the most successful folks in Three Rivers have graduated from Holy Assumption. Chief Bronson is one of them.

Old pictures online showed a college dorm building behind the school and a rectory to the left, between the school and the church. The dorm had been torn down after the college closed. The rectory was destroyed in a fire around the same time. A small house had been erected in that spot as the current priest's residence.

At five minutes to three, I drove down the alley behind the convent and parked Cricket on the concrete parking pad. No sign of the chief's Jeep Wrangler.

At precisely three o'clock, I went to the back door of the convent and knocked. Sister Celeste Marie herself answered the door, and I followed her into an office next to the dining room of the house.

I sat in the hard wooden chair in front of her desk. The chair probably guaranteed nobody would be sitting there long. I shifted from one cheek to the other.

The sister looked up at the wall clock and cleared her throat. "Erwin is late."

I looked at the clock. Five past three. "I texted Er—uh, I mean Chief Bronson. He didn't respond. He's on his way back from a hunting trip. I assume he's driving and ignoring his phone. Safety first, you know?"

She cleared her throat again. "Well, we can't wait for those who don't respect our time. Tell me what your plan is."

I swallowed hard and dove in. I confirmed that I'd be taking over Sister Mary Agnes's teaching duties, as requested. That would explain my presence at Holy Assumption. I told her I'd talk with the other sisters on a casual basis. "No rubber hoses or interrogations under hot lights," I said with a chuckle.

Sister Celeste Marie frowned. "Well, of course not! We're not criminals!"

"Sorry, Sister. I meant no offense. It was just a joke."

She gave me a long look, frowning deeper. "Is that what you think this is? A joke?"

I squirmed in the chair. She waited. The room got hotter. I squirmed again. "Absolutely not, ma'am, uh, Sister." I could see why the chief jumped when she came to TriMak.

Sister Celeste said, "I had my doubts about allowing you in, you know. But Erwin insisted on your being involved. I, reluctantly, agreed." She leaned toward me, eyebrows knit, speaking slowly, no doubt so the idiot before her could understand. "Don't make me regret that decision."

"Yes, Sister. I mean no, Sister. I mean, I won't, Sister."

She sat back and let out a sigh. "The police say Mary Agnes's death was an accident. I just want to be certain that is the case."

"Yes, Sister, that's why I'm here. As I said, I'd like to casually talk with the others, without arousing suspicion. Everything completely low-key. I have no desire to disrupt the convent or school routine."

Sister Celeste Marie nodded. "All right then. I'm pleased you understand how it must be while you're here." She glanced at the wall clock again.

I checked my phone. Nothing from the chief.

"Since it's obvious that Erwin is missing this meeting, we'll tour the facilities without him." She gestured to my cell phone. "That, of course, you'll need to set aside while you're here."

I said, "Um, I need to have access to the outside while I'm here." *Sounds like you're going to the slammer.*

"We *have* access," Sister Celeste said. She pointed to the landline telephone on her desk. "The sisters are free to use this telephone anytime. And we have an extension upstairs as well. The school, of course, has telephone access for communicating with parents. And the church and school even have websites. We are quite technologically minded here, for the sake of our students. But we sisters limit our use. I will expect you to do the same while you're here."

I agreed to keep the cell out of sight and on Do Not Disturb. But to not have it on my person felt, well, naked.

Sister Celeste said, "Besides, if the other sisters see you with a cell phone, it will no doubt 'blow your cover,' am I correct?"

I stifled a laugh.

She gave a tight smile. "We *do* watch television here on occasion, Ms. Prentice." She tilted her head at me. "On that note, obviously you can't use your own name, as you are known in the community." She explained that sisters are free to choose their own names as they enter religious life. Some keep their baptismal names.

"What about you? How did you become Sister Celeste Marie?"

"I took Saint Celestine's name, altered to Celeste. And Marie is for the Blessed Mother. Many of us take her name. Sister Mary Agnes, for example."

"Was Agnes her baptismal name?"

She shook her head. "Saint Agnes is the patron saint of young girls, chastity, and survivors of sexual abuse. So it's fitting that Sister Agnes dedicated her life to protecting and educating our girls, back when we were a women's college, and now as a co-ed high school." She gave me a long look, considering. "Let's see. What would be a good name for you while you're here?" She thought a moment. "Saint Michael is, I believe, the patron of law enforcement. Michelle would be the feminine of that."

"Hmm. Sister Michelle. I like it. Do I need a second name? Like Marie?"

"You can choose any second name you'd like."

"Is there a patron saint of detectives? Or investigators?" Before she could answer, I whipped out my cell and did a little Google magic. Boom. Instant results.

I said, "Saint Joshua is the patron saint of spies and intelligence experts."

Sister Celeste raised an eyebrow. I tried not to take that as a comment on what she thought of my intelligence.

I scrolled a little further down. Someone online facetiously suggested that a Saint Columbo was the patron saint of detectives. I chuckled to myself. I'm a huge fan of the old *Columbo* show on TV, and I often channel his trademark "Just one more thing" when he's talking to murderers.

I decided. "I've got it. I'll be Sister Michelle Columbo. Fits perfectly, don't you think?"

Sister Celeste Marie gave a quick nod, and with that, I was transformed from Mackenzie Prentice to Sister Michelle Columbo, undercover nun, spy, detective, investigator.

"Come now," Sister Celeste said. "We must prepare you to join the community."

CHAPTER NINETEEN

I FOLLOWED SISTER CELESTE UP the front staircase of the convent. The beautiful oak stairs were polished to a high sheen, as was the carved oak banister. Gram's Victorian has similar details, a testament to the craftsmanship in these old homes.

First stop was Sister Mary Agnes's room on the second floor. First impression: austere. Not quite the concrete-walled cells you see in the movie convents, but definitely austere. The scent of lavender hit me as I stepped into the room.

The plain white walls held only one decoration, an eight-by-ten-inch picture in a wooden frame on one wall. Jesus, holding a lamb. The frame hung slightly askew, but Little-Bit-of-OCD Me resisted the urge to straighten it.

One window, an ancient double-hung with its blue curtain pulled to each side, offered a view to the trees in the side yard of the convent, and beyond that a huge garden plot.

A small wooden rocking chair stood by the window, with another small table with a lamp. A crocheted blanket, white with a blue star pattern, was draped over one arm of the rocker.

I pictured the nun sitting there, praying or reading. A cozy little spot. I ran my hand across the blanket. "Did Sister Mary Agnes make this?"

She smiled. "Oh, yes. She loved to crochet. She made an afghan for each new sister who joined us. That is, she did until her arthritis made it painful. What a gift she had."

The neatly made twin bed was covered with a green-and-white-flowered duvet. A simple wooden table next to the bed held a small lamp with a white shade and a digital alarm clock. Next to the alarm was a small ceramic tray painted with a bluebird. The kind of tray you might have for earrings or for your spare change. *What did Sister Mary Agnes store there?*

Sister Celeste opened the closet, and the lavender scent wafted out, stronger. She gave a sad smile. "Mary Agnes loves lavender. We can always tell—" She stopped. "I mean, we *could* always tell when she was around. The scent . . ." She looked away. "I hope you don't find it unpleasant."

"On the contrary, Sister. It's nice. Reminds me of my grandmother."

Hanging on the closet rod were three gray skirts, six identical white blouses, and two gray cardigan sweaters that had seen a lot of wear. Several pieces of gray fabric attached to white headbands lay on the closet shelf—head coverings like the nun on the website was wearing.

"Here are her things. You look to be about her size. I'll wait in the hall while you change."

"Won't the other sisters wonder how I happen to be wearing the same, uh, uniform as she did? I'm supposedly coming from another place."

"Sisters are free to dress as they wish these days. You'll notice a variety of clothing when you meet the others. Sister

Mary Agnes's clothing is a very common choice among a variety of religious orders. No one will think anything about it, I'm sure."

I was stepping into another woman's life. A simpler, plainer life. I thought about a movie where a city-dwelling woman was sent to live with the Amish. Fish out of water. That was definitely how I felt at the moment.

I put on one of the white blouses and a gray skirt, then wriggled into a pair of Gram's pantyhose and slipped my feet into my black loafers. Final touch—a gray cardigan from Sister Mary Agnes's closet.

I looked at myself in the full-length mirror attached to the inside of the closet door. As the saying goes, "Clothes make the man." Well, they make the nun too.

"Ready, Sister," I said.

Sister Celeste came into the room and stood behind me. "One more thing. The veil," she said. She brushed my hair behind my ears, gently. I had a flash of memory, of Gram braiding my hair before school with that same gentle touch.

Sister Celeste set the headband of the veil over the crown of my head.

"Will it stay on?" I asked. I worried about the veil flying off if I had to chase a perp around the school.

"Oh yes, there is a metal headband inside the fabric," she said as she arranged the gray fabric that fell to my shoulder from the headband. She rested her hands on my shoulders and peered into the mirror. "Sister Michelle Columbo, welcome to Holy Assumption. May God grant you success." She patted my shoulders.

The memory of Gram combined with the sister's tenderness overwhelmed me, and I swallowed hard. *Professional investigators don't cry.* I looked at the floor. "Thank you, Sister. I'll do my best. I promise."

I turned around, and Sister Celeste gave me the once-over, head to foot. "You know, with a casual glance, you might be mistaken for Sister Mary Agnes."

"Um, wasn't she a lot older?"

"Well, okay, a *very* casual glance. Of course, she was a great deal older, and her hair was gray. But you're about the same height and build. Oh, and one last thing." She reached into her pocket and withdrew a rosary. "This belonged to Mary Agnes. I assume you don't have one of your own. We sisters keep our rosaries with us at all times. Keep it in your pocket."

Again, I felt touched. As I tucked it into the pocket of the cardigan, I fingered the beads, the chain, the crucifix, imagining the countless prayers the sister had prayed over her lifetime. I swallowed hard and looked at Sister Celeste. "I feel honored. And touched. This was precious to her."

She gave my arm a light pat. "Prayer is a powerful thing, Ms. Prentice. Perhaps her rosary will help guide your investigations. Now, Sister Michelle Columbo, let's continue our orientation."

CHAPTER TWENTY

I T WAS ALMOST 4:15 when Sister Celeste Marie and I walked down the back stairs to the main floor of the convent. No sign of the chief.

The back stairs were a stark contrast with the front stairs we'd taken earlier. This staircase was steeper, the painted wooden treads carrying slight indentations from decades—over a century—of feet traversing them.

I commented on the contrast, and Sister Celeste Marie said, "Yes, these are the servants' stairs. The back of the house— kitchen, butler's pantry, these stairs, the attic—all were the domain of the household staff years ago."

"I never imagined that nuns and priests would have servants."

"Well, that was *de rigueur* in those days. Not so many class distinctions anymore, of course. All large houses employed lay people to perform the household tasks." She explained that the attic of the convent had sleeping quarters in the past. "Now it is just storage, but back when the convent was full, novices slept in the attic."

I couldn't imagine how uncomfortable that would have been, in the hot summer in Three Rivers, sleeping in an attic before electric fans or air conditioning. Such wimps we are now.

We reached the main floor. I glanced at my phone. Nothing from the chief. I was on my own.

We walked through the dining room, past a small chapel, and into the front parlor of the convent. The convent and church had been built around the same time as Gram's Victorian, and the house felt very much like home to me.

Our tour took us back to the kitchen, at the back of the house, where I'd entered. A woman came out of a separate pantry. "Oh, here you are, Mrs. Jensen. This is Sister Michelle. She'll be with us until we find a permanent replacement for Sister Mary Agnes."

I looked up at the large woman—nearly six feet tall, broad shoulders, meaty arms. A white apron covered her gray print dress. I extended my hand. "Nice to meet you."

Mrs. Jensen hesitated, and I felt a wave of uncertainty. *Do nuns shake hands?*

Without meeting my eyes, she reluctantly took my hand. Strong grip. "Nice to meet you," she said softly.

Sister Celeste continued. "Mrs. Jensen is our cook and housekeeper. She's been with us for years and years. She and her husband have a home on the other side of the convent. And they have a lovely garden next door and provide all of our fresh summer produce. Our sisters help with the gardening. Sister Petronilla especially enjoys it." She turned. "Isn't that right, Mrs. Jensen?"

The housekeeper smiled, a light blush to her cheeks as she nodded. "Yes, Reverend Mother."

I said, "Very nice meeting you."

Mrs. Jensen gave a little curtsy. "Welcome, Sister. Anything you need, you let me know."

I thanked her, and she went back into the pantry.

Sister Celeste led me down the stairs to the basement of the convent. "We have a tunnel system here, connecting the convent to the church and to the school. Most useful in the cold weather. "This tunnel will take us to the church." She switched on the lights, illuminating a long hallway. The walls, ceiling, and floor were concrete. Sturdy. Bomb shelter sturdy. The tunnel was cool, and I pulled my—or rather Sister Mary Agnes's—cardigan closer.

Sister Celeste shared some of the church's history as we walked. We came to a flight of stairs, and at the top, another door opened into the front vestibule of Holy Assumption.

Our Savior's Lutheran is a lovely church, but this was spectacular. Soaring, three-story-high ceilings. Sunlight streaming through the huge round window above the front entry cast a kaleidoscope of color onto the polished marble floor. More stained-glass windows lined both sides of the sanctuary. The whole effect was one of light and, somehow, hope. Beautiful.

"You'll come to Mass each morning at 8:15 along with your homeroom students. Currently, we're sharing a priest with another parish—Father Joseph from Divine Conception."

"So Chief Bronson won't be doing Mass?"

"No, Erwin won't be celebrating the Mass, as he is not ordained. Did you know Erwin considered the priesthood?

Considering joining the priesthood and ending up as a cop? Quite the dichotomy. "I had no idea," I said. The chief and I have our own lives, and I realized we know very little about what goes on outside the office.

Sister Celeste Marie pointed to our left. "This way to the bell tower." We crossed the marble floor, and she opened the heavy, carved wooden bell tower door. "After you, Sister Michelle."

I almost laughed. Being a nun would take some getting used to. I stepped into the space. The round room with thick plastered walls had three heavy dark blue cords hanging from above. "Does someone ring the bells by hand?" The bells at Our Savior's were rung electronically. Gram had served on the fund-raising committee for the new system a few years back. Some systems didn't even have actual bells, just the bell sounds.

"We recently set things up electronically, but we're still getting used to it. Ringing the bells manually is still an option. The computerized system isn't reliable, but that might be operator error more often than not."

"Who runs the system?"

"That would be Mr. Jensen, our housekeeper's husband. He's the school custodian, maintenance man, and all-around helper." She gave a smile. "I can't imagine how we'd get along without the Jensens."

I noticed a folded blanket against the far wall of the alcove. Sister Celeste explained. "We leave blankets here for the unhoused people in the neighborhood. On cold nights, some find their way to us. We welcome them, following our Lord's direction to care for others. These people are in need. Of course, until we know for sure what happened to Sister Mary Agnes, we'll keep the church locked."

"Three Rivers has a homeless shelter. I would think that would be warmer, especially in the winter." Winter temperatures here can dive well below zero overnight. I couldn't imagine having to sleep outside any time of year, much less on a winter night.

"Some don't feel comfortable in a shelter."

"Is it possible one of them was here in the bell tower when Sister Mary Agnes fell?"

"It's possible, of course. But I'm not sure if that night was particularly cold. And the police found no evidence that anyone else was in the tower at that time."

"Do you know who these people are? Any names? Or where I might be able to find them?"

"One woman goes by the name of Harriet. And there's a man who calls himself Skip. And another we know as Archie. Of course, no telling if those are their real names."

I pulled out my phone and made notes, since my mental notes don't always stick around: Temperature that night? Harriet? Skip? Archie?

I looked up to see Sister Celeste frowning at me. "You must keep your phone hidden from the others. It will raise a great deal of suspicion among the other sisters and the students. We don't allow cell phones in school, and that applies to students and to staff. Of course, our lay teachers have their phones, but they keep them silenced and out of sight."

"I understand."

To the right, a curving concrete staircase led up, up, up three stories to the top of the tower. A wrought iron railing curved along the stairs. I saw light coming in through the large openings above. Spaces for the bell sounds to peal out over the town.

I took a few steps up the winding staircase, imagining that I was Sister Mary Agnes. "What would have drawn her up here?"

"She had cleaning duty in the sanctuary and would have

checked this lower area, but there would be no reason to ascend the stairs."

I thought about the OCD angle. "Was she a cleaning fanatic? Would she have been polishing this railing?" I pointed up. "Or dusting the bells?"

Sister Celeste's look told me how ridiculous my questions were. She shook her head. "Of course not."

"Okay, let's think this through. She comes into the bell tower for some reason. Maybe she heard something? Saw something? Here she is, for whatever reason, going up these stairs." I took four more steps upward, holding the wobbly railing. "This railing is loose."

"Yes, it's on the list of things to be repaired around here. It's a very long list."

I looked up and felt a little dizzy. "Could it be that she just got dizzy and fell? The police report said she took gabapentin. I looked that up, and it can cause dizziness and balance issues."

"Yes, she had gabapentin for her joint pain. Such bad arthritis. She had awful knees. That's a hazard for us, you know, since we spend so much time praying." She gave a little chuckle. Her face softened.

A joke? I smiled and took another step upward, then looked back. "Did she take anything else? Any other medication for pain?"

"Well, certainly not narcotics, if that's what you're implying!"

"Certainly not!" I echoed her indignation. My voice carried up the tower.

She went on. "We try to avoid prescription drugs, try to live a holistic life here, you know. Natural foods and organic vegetables, thanks to Mrs. Jensen. We value fresh air and exercise to keep us healthy, as the good Lord intended. Unfortunately, there are some things that all the praying in the world can't help. Mary Agnes suffered as long as she could before she capitulated to Big Pharma. If one of us truly needs something, it is allowed."

I came back down the stairs. "So she wasn't here to dust the bells. But she may have been checking the tower to be sure it was empty?"

Sister Celeste nodded. "I told the police that, and they seemed satisfied."

"Do *you* think someone else was in the tower? Perhaps lured her here?"

"A possibility, yes. But I have no evidence of that." She looked up at the top of the tower. "Just a feeling. Something wasn't right, but I don't know what. Call it divine intuition." Her voice went soft.

I bowed my head. It just felt like a prayerful moment.

Louder, she said, "That's why I asked Erwin for help."

I stifled a giggle. I'd never get used to hearing her—or anyone else—call the chief that. I looked at her.

She gave me that knit-eyebrowed scowl again. "This is not a laughing matter, Ms. Prentice!"

I immediately felt shame. "Sorry, Sister."

She raised herself to full height. "By the way, while you are here, you shall refer to me as 'Mother' or 'Reverend Mother.'"

I nodded. "Yes, Reverend Mother."

"Erwin insisted on involving you." She gave a little eye roll. *She does not like us much.* "I expect you to resolve this matter soon. We have a school to run, and the Halloween carnival is this week. So if there's nothing else, we'll return to the convent. Sister Petronilla will continue your orientation and answer any questions."

"Yes, Reverend Mother." I suppressed the urge to curtsy. I followed her back through the tunnel to the convent in silence.

CHAPTER TWENTY-ONE

SISTER CELESTE LEFT ME in the convent kitchen, and a moment later another nun came in. She smiled wide and said, "I'm Sister Petronilla, your tour guide and source of information. Welcome to Holy Assumption, Sister Michelle."

Dressed in a plain dark blue dress under a light blue cardigan, with no veil over her curls of fading red hair, she might have been just another woman on the street but for the lone indication of her vocation. A chunky wooden cross hung from a sash around her waist. She was short, maybe five-two, and in her mid-fifties by my guess. She had a gap between her top front teeth, and when she smiled, her face got all squinty and her green eyes danced. I liked her immediately.

According to the police report, Sister Petronilla was the last one to see the deceased. The investigator in me was itching to ask her all kinds of questions.

She asked if I wanted to freshen up before dinner. *Yes, please. It's been several hours since we last 'freshened up.'*

I followed her up the back stairs to the second floor. She

waited in the rocking chair in Sister Mary Agnes's room while I used the bathroom across the hall. I came back and sat on the edge of the bed.

Petronilla asked where I was from, and I spun the yarn that Reverend Mother and the chief had invented for me. How I'd been "stationed" at Holy Cross in Detroit and then taught high school at St. Mary's in Chicago. I told her I'd been on leave to care for my grandfather in Chicago for the past year before he died, and now I was ready to resume my teaching duties.

She told me how sorry she was about my grandfather.

I thanked her. "I was so sorry to hear about Sister Mary Agnes."

Sister Petronilla gave a sigh. "Mary Agnes was such a precious soul. We all miss her." She glanced away, looking out the window. "The community's loss is heaven's gain."

"Were you close?"

"Of course. The community is our family." She looked hard at me. "As you know." *Was there a hint of suspicion in her tone?*

I quick-stepped to steer the conversation back. "So sad that she fell."

Petronilla fingered a loose thread on her sweater sleeve. "Yes. So tragic. But we're all ready, aren't we?"

"Ready?"

She looked up. "Ready to be with the Lord, of course," she said with a smile. She looked so peaceful, so serene. *What's that like? To be so certain of eternity.*

I pressed forward. "Her falling down the stairs like that? What do you think happened?"

She hesitated, maybe deciding how much to say to this stranger. After a moment, she said, "She was old and getting frail. She had a bad hip. I wouldn't be surprised if her hip just gave out and she lost her balance and that's why she fell."

"Was it a usual thing for her to be in the bell tower like that?"

"Part of her duties. We all have our assignments, and we rotate through them. We check the tower every night." She leaned toward me and lowered her voice. "I saw her that night just before she went to the church. I told her to be careful. Sometimes we've found people—you know, vagrants—sleeping in the tower."

That answered my "what was she doing when you last saw her" question. "You kick the vagrants out?"

"Actually, we don't, even though it could be a safety issue for us. You never know."

Not the same charitable attitude Sister Celeste had expressed. "Do you think one of, uh, those people might have been there when Sister Mary Agnes fell?"

Petronilla thought a moment and then shrugged. "We assume she just collapsed in the tower, and the police don't suspect foul play."

"Why do you suppose she went up into the tower? Why go up the stairs like she did?"

"Perhaps she heard a noise, an animal maybe. We've had a terrible time with squirrels and bats, and once a huge crow built a nest up there. She may have noticed something like that and gone up to check."

Seemed plausible. "Do you have any reason to think anything might have been amiss for Sister Mary Agnes?"

The look on her face told me I'd asked one question too many. "Sister, you are welcome here, and we appreciate you taking over her classes. But her death is not something we want to dwell on. She is with our Lord now and at peace. And we must move on." *End of discussion.*

She swept a hand around the room. "Feel free to use anything here. We share everything. Waste not, want not, you know. Reduce, reuse, recycle."

Sister Petronilla was probably full of those old sayings. A stitch in time. A watched pot. All that old wisdom. If I started saying that stuff, Gram would be thrilled.

She went on to describe the morning routine. "Probably much like you're used to. We sisters tend to be a similar lot. Similar routines. You'll fit right in."

I couldn't explain that she didn't have a clue how challenging it would be for me to fit in, since I wasn't even Catholic. So instead, I said, "Well, I'm glad to have you as my guide. Things are all so new to me here."

Understatement of the century.

A bell sounded from downstairs. "That will be dinner," Petronilla said. As we went down the back stairs to the kitchen, she shared more of the routine. "Mrs. Jensen does the cooking. Breakfast during the week is hard-boiled eggs, fruit, and bread she prepares ahead of time. We serve ourselves. Weekdays, we eat lunch at the school—sandwiches or leftovers from the convent kitchen."

I remembered the cafeteria food at Three Rivers High. If we were lucky, one hot-lunch meal a week seemed edible, but the vanilla pudding was to die for. "What do the students eat?"

"They have the choice to bring their own lunch, or they can pay for a meal. We order ahead of time and have food delivered."

"Isn't that expensive?"

"For the students, certainly. But not providing cafeteria food saves us a lot of money. And since many of the older students drive, they are free to go off campus during the lunch hour."

Every night, dinner was at the convent dining room, prepared by Mrs. Jensen. "She's been here for eons. She does some light housekeeping for us as well. We are happy to have her, and she appreciates the small income we provide."

We reached the kitchen. The evening's dinner stood ready on the kitchen counter. Roast beef, mashed potatoes and gravy with green beans, with lemon meringue pie for dessert. All of it looked as good as Gram's, and trust me, that is high praise.

"This looks wonderful, as usual, Mrs. J."

Mrs. Jensen gave a nod.

Petronilla turned to me. "Nearly all the produce, from the potatoes to the green beans, comes from the garden next door. I help her in the garden, but Mrs. Jensen is the real green thumb."

Mrs. Jensen waved the compliment away. "Pshaw," she said.

Petronilla grabbed the platter of beef and headed to the dining room. I followed with the green beans, shiny with melted butter and sliced almonds. Mrs. Jensen carried in the mashed potatoes and gravy. We each set the dishes in the middle of the table.

Sister Celeste Marie, at the head of the table, waited until all were seated. Petronilla took the seat to Mother's left, and I sat next to Petronilla. Mrs. Jensen stood in the kitchen doorway.

Sister Celeste Marie bowed her head, and each nun followed suit. I peeked at the others and did a passable imitation of crossing myself. Sister Celeste led the prayer, beginning with, "Bless us, O Lord, for these thy gifts . . ." I breathed a sigh of relief. This prayer I knew from Gram.

With our "amen," the chattering began. Sisters passed dishes, oohing and aahing over the deliciousness of it all.

I glanced at Mrs. Jensen. She stood unsmiling.

Mother Superior stood and tapped her water glass with her knife. "Sisters, I'd like to introduce Sister Michelle Columbo to our community." Smiles all around the table directed toward me as she explained the whole thing about my filling in for Sister Mary Agnes. "Please make her feel welcome."

With that, the introductions began. To my left, Sister Rosemary Fontina, youngish, maybe mid-forties, teacher of faith traditions, whatever that meant.

Next to her, Sister Prudence Immaculata. She extended a hand behind Rosemary. I leaned back and shook it. Prudence said, "Great to have you here. I teach math, all levels. I've been here for ages, since the high school opened."

I scrutinized Sister Prudence's face. Other than her gray hair, she looked too young to have been at Holy Assumption for that long. Maybe all the praying kept wrinkles away. If so, I wanted to pray more often.

We leaned forward, and she continued. "That was such a great time in our history. So many amazing young women came through our doors. One of our graduates became a state senator. We get Christmas cards and updates from several of our alums." She lowered her voice. "One of them is a very generous donor."

"How nice."

"Yes, it's wonderful to see all they've accomplished. We are blessed to have been a small part of their lives."

Impressive.

Sister Doris Blackburn introduced herself from across the table. She wore a gray dress and vest, but the covering on her hair was bright pink. "I teach art and music. Perry Cuthbert taught art here back in the 1960s. Did you know that?"

I recognized the world-famous artist's name. "I knew he was from this area, but I didn't know he taught here."

Sister Doris grinned. "Yes! Perry is in his eighties now, but he comes back every year to offer a special workshop for the students. So generous with his time and talents."

"Has he been here recently?"

"Actually, he's here now—well, not *here*, but he's staying at the River View. He'll be in town until after Halloween.

Did he have anything to do with Mary Agnes's death? Add him to the list.

Sister Bernadette Clark was the last one across the table. School nurse, and substitute for sisters who are out ill or need to be away from Holy Assumption for whatever reason.

She'd found Mary Agnes's body that Sunday morning. I definitely had some questions for her. I just had to figure out a way to ask them.

Three empty chairs at the table. I whispered to Petronilla, asking who was missing. *Duh. The dead nun, maybe?* Snarky cuts me zero slack.

"Well, Sister Mary Agnes, of course. But you're in her chair."

A creepy something ran up my spine. The dead nun's clothes. Her room. Her classes. And now her seat at the table.

"We've had up to twelve, sometimes more, in our community. But fewer are entering the religious life these days." She gestured to the seat at the end of the table, opposite Sister Celeste. "That seat is reserved for the priest, when he chooses to join us."

I pictured the chief sitting there, if he ever showed up, and wondered again what was keeping him.

Sister Doris addressed Petronilla from across the table. "Please pass the gravy, Flowers."

"Flowers?" I asked.

Sister Petronilla laughed. "They call me Sister Mary Flowers because I work in the garden with Mrs. Jensen. I don't know who started it, but it stuck."

A younger woman had joined Mrs. Jensen in the doorway. I guessed her to be in her late forties but with this crowd, it was hard to guess ages. All that clean living, no doubt.

Sister Celeste announced, for my benefit. "Mrs. Jensen has a kitchen helper, her daughter Hannah."

Hannah Jensen brought a pitcher of water to the table, refilling glasses as she made the circuit, beginning with Mother Superior, then Petronilla. As she extended the pitcher toward my glass, Petronilla bumped her elbow, and Hannah sloshed water onto the tablecloth in front of me.

She gave a gasp and grabbed my napkin to mop it up.

Petronilla laid a hand on Hannah's arm and steadied her. "It's all right, Hannah. Don't worry. This is Sister Michelle Columbo."

Hannah stared at me with piercing gray eyes a moment before giving me a quick smile, saying nothing.

"Nice to meet you, Hannah," I said.

She nodded, then finished refilling water glasses and went out to the kitchen.

"She doesn't speak much," Sister Rosemary whispered. "She's a little slow, but she does a fine job. Lovely girl."

I added Mrs. Jensen and Hannah to my mental list of inter-viewees. Perhaps they'd seen or heard something, or someone, the night the nun died.

We chatted on through dessert. Sister Petronilla explained that after dinner, we'd have quiet contemplation time for half an hour, and then sisters were free from seven until nine to do whatever they wished. More quiet time from nine until 10:00 p.m. lights out.

"Want to explore a little? We can meet at seven, and I'll show you the tunnels."

Ooh, an adventure! I agreed.

CHAPTER TWENTY-TWO

I WENT UPSTAIRS TO MY—UH, Mary Agnes's room—for my version of "quiet contemplation." I sat on the edge of the bed and gave it a little bounce. The mattress was not too firm, not too soft. Just right. I propped the two pillows against the headboard and stretched out on the bed.

I checked for texts from the outside world. Nothing from the chief. *Where the heck are you, Erwin?* I sent him a text to that effect, without the "Erwin," of course.

I'd gotten a text from Heather Sullivan.

> Mtg guy Tuesday 7pm Donatellos. U back me up?

It took a second to register. *Oh yeah. Heather's "attorney," who "worked weekends."* Snarky let the air quotes fly.

If I was supposed to be doing nun things at seven Tuesday night, when Heather needed me, I'd make some excuse to go help her. That's what friends do.

I texted back a thumbs up with:

> U text n I'll be there

I closed my eyes, thinking about the case. Mrs. Marberry had hinted about something unforgivable, a burden her sister carried. What was it? Was that burden simply too much to carry any longer? What if Sister Mary Agnes went up those stairs to hurt herself? To hang herself up there? Or to jump out of the tower and smash herself onto the concrete?

Or maybe Sister Mary Agnes was having a particularly painful day and took extra medication. Maybe that caused drowsiness or caused her to lose her balance on those steps. Maybe the railing wobbled at the wrong moment.

I had only questions, no answers. I wanted to go back into the bell tower and check it again, alone this time. I do my best thinking that way. Alone.

I picked up the paper schedule Sister Celeste had given me.

DAILY SCHEDULE

6:00 a.m. Wakeup.

6:30 Meditation and prayer.

7:00 Breakfast.

7:30 School prep time.

8:00 Students arrive for homeroom.

8:15 to 8:45 Mass.

9:00 Classes begin.

Noon Lunch.

1:00 to 3:00 Classes.

3:00 After school activities

5:00 Prayer and meditation.

6:00 Dinner.

6:30 Quiet contemplation.

7:00 Free time/recreation.

9:00 Quiet hour.

10:00 p.m. Lights out.

The days were pretty well set for the community. Little-Bit-of-OCD Me loved that predictability. Everything in its place. That applied to every*one* as well.

That was the sister side of things. Petronilla had filled me in on the teaching side.

Students assemble in homerooms at 8:00. Attendance, announcements, then move as a class to the sanctuary for Mass at 8:15. Homerooms sit together and then go back to the school for the first class at nine.

Classes were fifty minutes long with a ten-minute break in between. Just like our schedule at Three Rivers High back in the day. Just enough time between classes for a quick bathroom break, or in the case of Billy and me, time to make out in a stairwell.

My first class would be juniors at ten, then a ninth and tenth grade combo at eleven. Lunch for everyone from noon to one. Lunchroom monitoring appeared to rotate. I was exempt since I was new, Petronilla said, so my schedule was open from noon until two daily. I'd be free to snoop around, maybe interview people outside the convent and school. Then I was scheduled to monitor a study hall at two each afternoon until school was dismissed at three. Done for the day.

Busy, busy, busy. I closed my eyes, trying hard to imagine myself as a teacher. I dozed off. Sister Petronilla's knock woke me just after seven. She stood at the door in jeans and a sweatshirt, a flashlight in her hand. "Ready to explore?"

I was still in my skirt and blouse. I thought about changing into my sweats but decided not to. I thought about taking out my TriMak flashlight, but I didn't want to raise my tour guide's suspicions. "Ready!" I said and gave her a little salute.

"Do you have a jacket? The tunnels can be chilly, especially at night."

My only jacket was my TriMak windbreaker. I dug through Bob and put on the black hooded sweatshirt.

I closed the door behind me. A woman I hadn't seen before was in the hallway. She looked to be a hundred years old, her skin so thin, almost transparent. Decades of experience, wisdom were etched into her face. She wore a long, white nightgown as she shuffled toward the bathroom, supporting herself with a walker.

Petronilla whispered, "This is Mother Angeline. She was our Superior long ago." To the old nun she said, loudly, "Good evening, Mother."

The old woman looked at Sister Petronilla for a long moment. I read confusion in her eyes, then recognition. "Good evening, dear," she said. She looked at me. "Mary Agnes, you're looking well."

Obviously her eyes were going.

I started to correct her but Petronilla put a restraining hand on my arm. "Do you need any help, Mother?"

"Oh no, dear, you go about your business. I'll be fine."

We left her heading into the bathroom. Petronilla explained as we headed to the church tunnel. "Angeline is our retired Mother Superior. Been here for decades. And very forgetful at times. But she's in good health. Just some memory issues, but what do we expect at nearly a hundred years old?"

I thought about Nathan's "memory issues" and how Gram encourages us to just "be where he is" rather than trying to correct him. I lied and told Petronilla that the fictitious grandfather I'd been caring for before coming to Holy Assumption had had memory issues as well.

"You know how it is, then," Petronilla said with a smile. "We just go with the flow. Angeline joins us for meals or eats in her room if she prefers. We spend time with her each day. She mistook you for Mary Agnes. You are about the same height and build."

Sister Celeste had said the same thing to me.

"She gets around very well considering her age. There's a bell in her room that rings in the upstairs hall and also downstairs if she needs any help."

I followed Petronilla down to the kitchen and through the basement to the tunnel to the church. I told her that Sister Celeste had taken me this far before.

"Did you see the labyrinth?"

I shook my head. She led me into another section of the church basement and turned on lights. A massive circle of red and yellow tiles, curving around and back on itself, covered the floor. The pattern reminded me of a human brain or a giant snail.

"This was laid at the time the church was built. For decades, religious have walked this, praying."

"It's beautiful," I said again. A sense of peace, of history, filled the space.

"We sisters come here often. Very meditative, very contemplative. You'll love it."

I promised her I'd try it.

Sister Petronilla checked her watch. "Let's go on, then," she said. We left the labyrinth and rejoined the tunnel to the school. Halfway through, another tunnel extended to the left, barricaded with a sawhorse, a DO NOT ENTER sign and a blue tarp hanging behind it.

"What's down there?" I asked.

"We'll check that on the way back. Let's go to the school first."

We reached the end of the tunnel. Petronilla turned on the lights, and the school's basement hallway was illuminated. She pointed out the music room and lunchroom on the basement level. We looked into the gym. "This is where we'll have the carnival on Friday. The kids love it. Mary Agnes's classroom is on the second floor." She pointed above our heads. "I mean *your* classroom. Do you want to go up and see it?"

I shook my head. "My first class is at ten tomorrow morning. I'll go early to check it out."

"Students will be there for homeroom at eight. Then we have Mass. You'll want to plan accordingly."

"Of course," I said, keeping my tone casual, as if planning for Mass and teaching were completely natural for me. Instead of terrifyingly unnatural.

She turned off the school basement lights, and we headed back to the sawhorse barrier. "We're raising the money to close off this tunnel since it just leads to the old dorm and rectory. The carnival this year should bring in enough money for us to seal it. But this year, the seniors wanted to make it a haunted tunnel kind of thing. A new addition to the carnival."

I said, "I'm kind of surprised the school would even have a Halloween carnival. It's such a secular holiday."

Petronilla gave me a long look. I swallowed hard. I'd blundered. *If you were a* real *sister, you'd know.*

She frowned. "As I'm *sure* you know," she said, a question in her tone, "it's the eve of All Saints' Day, a decidedly Christian holiday."

Snarky snarked. *Duh. All Hallows' Eve. Halloween. Idiot!* I laughed and faked it. "Of course, I know that! I've just never encountered this kind of thing anywhere else that I've been, uh, . . ."—*Oh, what's the word the chief used? Oh yeah!*—"stationed."

She paused, considering, then nodded. I hoped that meant she bought it.

She pushed the tarp aside and hit the switch to turn on the three dim ceiling bulbs. "Reverend Mother thought the haunted tunnel idea was a bit over the top, but the students really wanted to try it. This tunnel is usually dark to discourage the students from coming down here."

Golly gee, high schoolers in the dark. Whatever would they be doing? Billy and I met in many a dark corner for between-class kissing. *Where there's a will.*

I followed Petronilla and, just beyond the ceiling illumination, we came to a fork in the tunnel. She turned on her flashlight, a puny little number that offered a weak circle of light. She gestured with the flashlight to the right. The beam hit a concrete wall. "That went to the old college dorm. The dorm was torn down just after the college closed." She swiveled the light to the left. The space was open, dark, and seemed to go on forever. "This is the old rectory tunnel. C'mon."

This part of the tunnel felt colder than the others. I rubbed my upper arms as I hugged myself, following Petronilla. "What happened to the old rectory?"

"It burned later the same year the college closed. The current priest's residence is that small house behind the church."

I wondered if the chief would be staying there this week. Assuming he showed up at all.

I noticed three wooden doors on the right side of the tunnel, one padlocked. "What's behind these doors?"

"Storage, mostly in the past. Nobody uses them anymore. I'm sure they're empty."

I didn't say what I was thinking, that an empty storeroom wouldn't need a padlock. We headed forward to a set of stairs that ended at ceiling height. "Stairs to the old rectory," she said. "But check this out."

She stepped a few feet to the left and shone the light. The light disappeared into a large hole in the tunnel wall above a knee-high concrete block wall. Two parallel wooden boards had been fastened over the hole, but one of them hung loose. I smelled stagnant water and heard dripping from somewhere above our heads. We stepped to the wall, and Petronilla swept the light around the concrete walls of the space. I guessed it to be maybe eight to ten feet square, and maybe eight to ten feet high.

"This is the old cistern that supplied water to the rectory. Back in the old days, rainwater filled it. It was sealed up at one point, but the rains and snow melt over the last couple years have leaked into the cistern. We're raising the money to have it drained and closed off permanently."

I took a whiff of the swampy water. "Smells awful. No telling what's living in there."

Petronilla laughed. "Since you teach biology, you can find out."

"No thanks," I said.

A metal ladder hung on the right side of the cistern. I took a guess. "Maybe that ladder was for maintenance?"

"I believe so. There's an access hatch outside above the ladder. In the rectory yard."

Just as Lillian Sharp had said. Every snoopy, nosy, curious part of me wanted to climb that ladder. Rational Me didn't want to arouse suspicion. "Any idea how deep the water is?"

She laughed. "Nope. I've never been tempted to take a swim."

I asked, "Does everybody know about this?"

She used a spooky, quavering tone. "Only those of us *brave* enough to explore. Whoo-ooo . . ." She gave a ghostly laugh, then got serious. "It's not safe. We need to seal this tunnel off before some student ends up drowning." She pointed the light at her watch. "We should probably get back."

As we turned to go, I thought I heard a moan. Rational Me had an explanation. *The wind, no doubt. Coming from outside, probably from the cistern access above. No doubt.*

Then another moan. I grabbed Petronilla's arm. "That's gotta be the wind, right?"

She put her hand on my arm and ran her fingers up my sleeve. "Whoo-ooo! Welcome to Spook Central." She laughed and so did I, but we both walked a little faster back to the convent.

CHAPTER TWENTY-THREE

I T WAS ALMOST MIDNIGHT and all quiet on the convent front. I wanted to check the bell tower by myself. I got out of bed, zipped my black hoodie over my pajama top, slid into black sweatpants, and put on thick white crew socks. I took out my TriMak heavy-duty flashlight from Bob.

I carried my ASICS—I didn't want any squeaking on the hardwood floor to waken anyone—and padded in my stocking feet down the back stairs to the kitchen. I put on my shoes, then stepped out the back door.

The night air was cold, and the wind had an extra bite to it. Gram would say, "Smells like snow." We don't usually get much snow before Halloween, but you never know. A wicked wind whipped around me. I'd planned to do a quick sprint across the yard to the front doors of the church but nixed that idea. The church would be locked, Sister Celeste had said, since a stranger off the street might have had something to do with Mary Agnes's death.

I ducked back inside the kitchen, then down to the tunnel. I flicked the light switch, and three bare bulbs hanging from the ceiling lighted the way.

Amazing how creepy a place can feel at night. "Spook central," Sister Petronilla had said.

I trotted the length of the tunnel from the convent, my shoes squeaking along the way. Upon reaching the far door, I took the steps up to the church vestibule. Wall sconces lent dim light to the space.

I paused, listening. The only sound was the wind outside. I went to the bell tower door on tiptoe. It seemed sacrilegious somehow to squeak and disturb the silence in the church. I pulled on the wooden door. It didn't move. I yanked harder, and it came open. The wind coming through the open area above obviously created a vacuum. I stepped into the tower. The door closed behind me with a rush, making a loud thunk as the tower sucked it closed. I waited, listening.

Silence, but for a murmur of wind. I shivered, wishing I had a heavier sweatshirt or my TriMak jacket.

The wind gave an eerie moan from above, sounding almost human. *Was this what you heard, Sister? Did this draw you up the stairs?*

I stepped up three stairs and paused. The high whine of wind coming through the openings at the top of the tower might be mistaken for a cry. Mary Agnes may have been confused that night. Perhaps she imagined this was someone calling for help.

I moved farther up the stairs, halfway to the bells. The wind calmed and then blasted again, louder as I moved upward. Another stronger gust of wind, this one blowing down the steps toward me, as if the stairwell were suddenly a wind tunnel. I gripped the railing harder.

What if a blast of wind hit her and she lost her grip? Possible. Possible. Possible.

I continued up and saw three heavy iron bells attached to a thick wooden bar, with long ropes hanging down to the floor below. Just as you'd expect in a church tower.

With another strong whoosh of wind, a flash of lightning illuminated the space. Suddenly, the bells rang and then rang again. Was someone pulling the ropes? Or had lightning affected the electronic system?

The bells reverberated through the tower, through my body. I took my hands off the railing and covered my ears. I turned and started down the steps, covering one ear and holding the flashlight with the other hand. No third hand to grasp the railing.

I pointed the flashlight beam into the space below and hollered, "Is someone there?"

No answer. I took a few more steps, shining the light downward. I thought I saw the door to the vestibule open, then close. Had someone been there, or were my eyes playing tricks? The vibrations of the bells calmed as I eased my way down. I could imagine an old woman up here, with bad knees, a bad hip, maybe on medication, easily losing her balance and tumbling down these steps.

I reached the alcove. The ropes moved slightly. Was it just the wind, or were they settling down after being pulled?

I hustled back to the tunnel, to the kitchen, and took the back stairs two at a time to the second floor. I paused halfway up. Lights were on in the hall above. I tucked the flashlight under my hoodie and finished the climb.

The sisters—Petronilla, Rosemary, Bernadette, Prudence, and Doris—were chattering in the hall in their robes. I guessed Mother Angeline hadn't heard the commotion.

Sister Bernadette looked me up and down. "Did you hear the bells?"

"Yes," I said, taking a breath to calm myself. Then I told a big fat lie to explain my outfit. "I, uh, couldn't sleep. My stomach was upset, so I got a little water with baking soda and then went outside. Fresh air helps."

Snarky whispered, *Special place in hell for you, lying to nuns.*

Sister Bernadette went into school nurse mode. "Are you feeling better now?" She felt my forehead. "No fever." Such concern for my welfare. Such tenderness in her touch.

I felt guilty for lying. Snarky was probably right about going to hell, but it couldn't be helped.

Sister Celeste Marie came up the back stairs in her robe. Odd to see her out of uniform. "I just spoke with Mr. Jensen. He said he heard the bells and came right over. He checked the system and thinks the lightning must have jolted something." She clapped her hands. "Let's get back to bed, all of us."

She raised an eyebrow at me, probably wondering why I was dressed as I was, but she said nothing.

I was almost back to sleep when my cell buzzed. A text from the chief:

> Had car trouble. Be there in AM.

About time you showed up, Erwin.

CHAPTER TWENTY-FOUR

DON'T KNOW WHEN I'VE felt more nervous. Not on a prom night. Not before exams in college. My stomach was in a knot at eight o'clock Monday morning as my classroom—room 212—filled with fifteen students—six boys and nine girls. Homeroom time.

I'd written "Sister Michelle Columbo" on the whiteboard. In movies and on TV, that's what the teacher does. Introductions via whiteboard.

I took attendance. Scott Lawrence, Lucy Lindstrom, Amanda McCall, Kimberly Morris, Garrett Nance. I sensed a theme. Ah, yes. Students were assigned to homerooms alphabetically. I went through the whole list. They all seemed perfectly nice, but I remembered how high school could be. Cliques and rivalries and such, to say nothing of all those raging hormones.

At 8:00 a.m. these kids seemed exceptionally quiet. Snarky reminded me, *Remember? High schoolers are half asleep at this hour. Don't let your guard down.*

I looked at them. *Were we this young in high school?* They were all neatly dressed, all in compliance with the dress code I'd seen online. Faces clean, hair combed. Respectful demeanors.

I heard a scuffle from the back row and looked up as one of the girls swatted at the boy across the aisle from her desk. I stood, frowned, and cleared my throat loudly. "Ahem! Is there a problem back there?" Sister Celeste had advised me not to smile, so as to establish my authority.

The girl said, "He's being rude, Sister." She pointed at the red-haired boy next to her.

I looked at the attendance list again. "Garrett Nance, right?"

He pointed at the girl. "*She* started it."

I looked at her. "Lucy Lindstrom, correct?"

"Yes, Sister." She looked at him. "And I did not!"

Garrett: "Did too!"

Lucy: "Did not!" She stuck out her tongue.

I clapped my hands. "Both of you stop this instant! I expect to hear this kind of thing from little children on the playground. You people are too old for this nonsense." I heard an echo of my high school algebra teacher, Miss Madigan. She always referred to us as "you people."

Lucy and Garrett offered me apologies. Mumbled, but apologies, nonetheless. I channeled Gram, who had intervened in many a childhood squabble among us siblings. "Now shake hands!"

Lucy rolled her eyes, then extended her hand. Garrett shook it. Lucy made a big display of wiping the hand on her blouse.

Garrett mumbled something.

Lucy yelled. "Sister! He just called me a—"

I held up a hand. "Enough!" I said, a near-shout. The same voice I would use to yell "stop" at a fleeing suspect. If I were a cop. If I weren't pretending to be a nun. *Do nuns yell?* The sisters I'd met so far seemed quiet and reserved, and certainly in control of their tempers. If they even *had* tempers.

Duh. Of course they do. They're human, aren't they? Snarky is pretty sure she knows everything.

The class got quiet. I checked the schedule. "Time for Mass," I said. The students stood, silently, lined up, and single-filed it out of the room.

Impressive. Very impressive.

Back in room 212 after Monday's Mass, the students had moved on to their first classes, and I had an open hour before I began to teach. I opened the materials. Subject: Sexuality Education. The curriculum included units for grades nine through twelve. Over seventy-five lessons in total.

Anxious Me felt a familiar knot in the stomach. *Have mercy. We'll never survive that long.*

According to my predecessor's notes, she'd already covered the first sections—anatomy, puberty, adolescent development. *Thank goodness!* Sister Mary Agnes had no doubt already endured the whispers, smirks, and snickers about those topics.

On tap for today: Pregnancy and Reproduction. *Oh boy.* I know zip about pregnancy, since I've never been. From what I've witnessed with my sister and sister-in-law, the whole thing seemed painful and very messy.

At ten, I had a classroom full of juniors. I recognized Lucy and Amanda from my homeroom. Others introduced themselves. Megan, with red hair and glasses. Kelsey, who had brown braids and braces. Lucy Lindstrom appeared to be the leader of the pack—outspoken, confident.

On the whiteboard under my name, I wrote "Pregnancy and Reproduction." I turned back from the board and pointed to a girl in the front row who had her hand in the air.

"Since I don't know you, please say your name and then ask your question."

"I'm Janine Bradshaw." She gave me a bright smile and a look of encouragement, with kindness in her eyes. Maybe this would be okay. Maybe I could count on her support.

With great effort, I resisted smiling back. *Don't let them think you're a pushover.* Miss Madigan never smiled, and she had our classroom under control. Not smiling sets the right tone. *Me teacher, you student. I make rules. You follow them.*

"Do you have a question?"

Janine's smile faded. "No, I just wanted to tell you it's nice to have you here, especially after Sister Mary Agnes."

"Meaning what?" My voice sounded a little sharper than I intended.

Janine blushed. "Just that I—we—hope you're not going to be as strict as she was."

"Strict? What do you mean?"

"Just that she was so—"

Lucy jumped in. "She was a real B, you know?"

I smacked my hand against my desk. "Lucy Lindstrom, we will use *proper* language in this classroom." I cringed inwardly. *Hypocrite.* I looked at their faces as I searched for words that would sound sister-like. "And we *certainly* will not speak ill of the dead." *Ah, yes. Very nunnish.*

Lucy gave a toss of her head. "Sorry, Sister." She glanced at her classmates. "But she *was.* Right, girls?"

The others nodded in agreement. Had the late sister made an enemy in this group? Someone angry enough to cause her bodily harm?

I shifted into investigator mode. "Did Sister Mary Agnes have any enemies? Anyone mad enough to fight with her?"

No one spoke. "Well, if anyone wishes to speak with me privately, I'm always available. Now let's get on with today's lesson."

Teaching turned out to be a lot easier than I thought it would be. Students took turns reading the material aloud. I posed questions, right there in the teacher's guide, and they discussed in groups of three. They discussed; I relaxed. After half an hour, the groups shared their thoughts.

Easy peasy lemon squeezy.

At the end of class, assigning homework elicited the same groans I remembered from my school days. *How dare these teachers infringe on our free time? Don't we ever get a break?*

"Are there any questions?"

I heard lots of whispering, "Ask her. Ask her," from the back of the room.

"Is there a question?"

"Yes, Sister." Lucy Lindstrom again. "We saw Miss Murdock and Mr. Sanborn out in his car after school. What were they doing?"

The whole class snickered. I could only imagine what the two teachers might have been doing. I put on my sternest nun expression. "Perhaps they were talking about which ones of you were going to be failing their classes. I might join that conversation next time."

The snickering stopped.

Snarky said, *Well played.*

Indeed.

A bell chimed, and the students filed out of the classroom, complaining about the homework I'd assigned.

Janine hung back, and when we were alone, she came to my desk. "Sister, um, I don't know if I should say anything or not."

"About what, Janine?"

"It's just that some of the girls were upset with Sister Mary Agnes, and the grades they got on the midterm exams in this class and in biology."

"Who was upset?"

She shook her head. "I can't say."

"You *can't* say, or you *won't* say?"

She gave me an apologetic smile. "Anyway, just wanted you to know." She left the room.

Know what exactly? Kids were upset with their grades? Big whoop.

At the end of my 11:00 class, students left grumbling about homework, as the previous group had. A thin girl, on the short side with red hair and glasses, stayed behind.

"Sister, can I talk to you?"

I sat behind the desk. Snarky resisted correcting her grammar with, *I don't know if you* can, *but you* may. *Are we talking about ability or permission? Miss Madigan would be so proud.*

I nodded at her. "Certainly. It's Megan, right?"

"Yes. I just wanted to say I'm glad you're here. There are so many rumors going around about what happened to Sister Mary Agnes. You being here means we can all just move on."

My investigator senses tingled. "What kind of rumors?"

Megan looked right and left and lowered her voice. "That she, you know, jumped from the bell tower. Or that—even worse—someone *murdered* her." Her eyes got wide. "*Did* someone murder her?"

I sat back, tented my fingers, and gave her my wisest look. "There are always unfounded rumors in a case—uh, a situation like this. I'm sure there is a perfectly logical explanation for her death. The important thing is that we move on."

Megan raised an eyebrow. "And pray for her and for her family, right, Sister?"

I felt heat rise in my cheeks. *Some nun you are*, Snarky said. "Of course, of course. That goes without saying." Anxious whispered, *Nice recovery.*

I looked at Megan. "Where do you need to be next?"

Megan headed to her algebra class.

I needed to go meet Officer Samantha Dutton at Hilda's Cafe. I stood up to leave as the chief came in and closed my classroom door behind him.

He said, "Glad I caught you between classes."

CHAPTER TWENTY-FIVE

RECOGNIZED THE VOICE BUT not the man. Black suit, black shirt, white clerical collar. Gold wire-rimmed glasses. The man does love a disguise. He'd darkened his hair and slicked it back and added a dark mustache and a short beard from the costume closet in his office at TriMak. He'd overdone it with the eyebrows, which looked like two black woolly bear caterpillars stuck to his forehead. (Gram would say those eyebrows—like the real woolly bears—were predicting a harsh winter.)

I snapped at him. "Where the hell have you been?"

He clucked his tongue. "Tsk, tsk. Language, Sister. It's a long story. I'm here now. My cousin Benedict lent me the suit. What do you think? Can I pass for a priest?"

"As well as I pass for a nun."

He checked my outfit and veil and raised the woolly bears. "You fit the part perfectly."

"Thanks, I think."

"I'm calling myself Father Percival."

"And I'm Sister Michelle Columbo."

He gave a chuckle. "Columbo? Hilarious. So catch me up. What do you have so far?"

"I checked the bell tower. It's plausible that it was accidental, like the cops said. I've met the sisters. No one stands out there. I had two classes this morning. Evidently, some animosity among the students toward Mary Agnes about grades or strictness in general. I'll dig further."

The chief frowned. "That's pretty slim. Kid gets a bad grade, so they kill the teacher?"

I shrugged. "I agree, but it would have had to be an accident. Also, there are some homeless people who may have been around that night. A woman named Harriet, someone they call Skip, and this guy Archie. I'm going to try and track them down."

"I can do some checking too. If it's the same Archie I know, he's not going to be a reliable witness. Guy's pretty messed up."

"Worth checking him out, though, right? If last Saturday night was cold, one of those people might have been inside the church. What if Sister Mary Agnes startled them and they attacked her for some reason?"

"I don't recall any of them being violent, but it's worth checking, yeah. Anyone else?"

"Could you give a call to a Doctor Finlay—he signed off on the death report. I assume he's at Our Lady of Mercy."

"Check," he said. "You like anyone as a suspect yet?"

"At this point, nobody and everybody. Seems the sisters all get along very well. And the housekeeper, daughter, and her husband—he's the custodian here—are well loved. It's all just one big happy family."

"Yeah. Until it's not. Keep digging. We've got to be sure about this one. For everyone's peace of mind."

I said, "I have another concern. Having to keep our cell phones on silent and out of sight is harder than I thought." No texting? No instant connections? Like living in the Stone Age. "How will you and I connect with each other? What if we get into trouble with this case and need help?"

"Good point," the chief said. "Hell to be without access to connection."

"*Hell?* Seriously, Chief? Didn't you grow up disconnected? Seems like people got along okay back then before we were connected 24-7."

He chuckled. "Yeah, okay, maybe it's not 'hell,' but it is a challenge. We need to figure out how to connect if we need to. You never know what direction a case might take."

"What would you suggest? Bat signal?"

"Chicken signal," he said and snorted.

"Very funny. Seriously, what can we do?"

"Keep your cell on vibrate and tuck it in your underwear."

"Okay, so let me see how that would work. I'm standing in front of the class, and my undies start vibrating. How exactly do you suggest I deal with that? In front of a bunch of teenagers?"

He frowned. "Yeah, I see your point. How about this? We put location trackers on our phones. I can see where you are at all times, and vice versa. And if we need help—"

I held up a hand. "I'm not sure I want you to know where I am at all times. We should be able to disable the trackers when we're not working on this case."

"Agreed."

"Good. So, I know where you are, but how do I know if you need help? How do I know if you've texted me?"

He thought a moment, then held out his left wrist. "You have one of these?" A fitness tracker.

"Nope. My mom has one, monitoring her heart rate, her steps, her workouts, and even her sleep. Seems like overkill to me. Just because we *can* track something doesn't mean we *should.*"

"I have an older one at home you can use. It's like wearing a watch, so it won't arouse suspicion. I'll set it up for you so you'll get notified if you get a text. Vibrates on the wrist. Easy to take a look, even when you're in class. You can read the text and respond, but only limited to an autoreply, just a word or two, built into it."

"Genius." We left my classroom and headed down the hall.

Mr. Jensen, mopping a spill in front of some lockers, looked up as we passed. "Good afternoon, Sister. Father," he said with a nod. Then he squinted at the chief. "I know you, don't I, Father?"

The chief looked away, covered his mouth, and gave a little cough. Voice lower, he said, "No, I don't think so. I just got here this week. On my way to California." *Liar.*

Mr. Jensen gave his head a little shake. "Huh. I know I've seen you before. I don't usually forget a face."

The chief glanced up and chuckled as he raised the woolly bears. "I get that all the time. I have that kind of face. People always telling me I look like someone they know."

Mr. Jensen shrugged and went back to mopping as we walked away.

"Close one," I said.

"I thought for sure Doc recognized me."

"Doc?"

"Yeah, he's been here forever, before I was in high school. We called him Doc because he can fix anything, from sprained ankles to plugged toilets to broken hearts. Kids confide in him.

He's just a helluva nice guy. He might make the connection, so let's watch ourselves."

I left the chief—rather, Father Percival—in front of the church, got into Cricket, and headed to Hilda's.

OFFICER DUTTON WAS ALREADY AT THE café, in running clothes, eating a roast beef sandwich. I ordered a blueberry muffin, then explained why I was undercover at the convent. "You were first on the scene, right? Can you tell me your impressions?"

Dutton told me how she'd found Sister Mary Agnes's body. "It was obvious she'd fallen down the stairs."

"Any sign of anyone else there?"

She shook her head and frowned. "No, I would have put that in my report."

"Of course. But you know how it is. We see things, know things and don't realize it. Anything at all?"

She paused, chewing as she looked at the ceiling. "I didn't think anything of it at the time, but there was mud."

"That wasn't in the report. How much mud? Where?"

She shrugged. "Like you said, you see things and they don't register until later. There was dried mud on the floor by the body and some on the stairs."

"Was there mud on the nun's shoes?"

"No. They weren't muddy. Someone off the street tracked it in. It was dried. Probably there for days. That's my guess. I'm sure it was nothing. If I thought it mattered, I'd have amended the report." She said she had to get to work.

"Well, if you think of anything, text me, okay?" I gave her my cell number.

She promised she would, then said, "You make a great nun. If I didn't know better, I'd swear you were legit."

"Bless you," I said.

She laughed and then took off. I wrapped the rest of the muffin in a napkin, paid the check, and left Hilda's. Jimbo chirped when I started Cricket. I tossed him a piece of muffin and talked aloud to him all the way back to Holy Assumption.

"Mud? What's that about, Jimbo? Persons unknown came in off the street and left mud behind? I can understand mud at the bottom of the tower, but at the top of the stairs? You come in for a rest, so yeah, you track mud into the alcove. But why would you climb the stairs?"

Jimbo had no clue.

Half an hour later, back at the school, the chief and I had instant connectivity via our phones and trackers. He'd also brought a charging cord. "Be sure to keep the tracker charged up. I gave this older one a little jolt, but it needs to fully charge, since I haven't been using it. Give it a couple hours, and we should be good to go."

I summarized our plan. "So, we will track each other's location with our phones. We'll text if we need help. The text will show on the wrist device. We check the phone to see where the other person is. Is that it?"

He nodded. "Yes. You'll text me if you need help, and I'll check your location and race to the rescue. Like always."

I laughed. "Ha! As I recall, you show up after I've done the dirty work."

He shrugged. "Hey, I can't help it if you like to go it alone. I've told you time and again to wait for the cavalry before you charge into dangerous situations. But do you listen to me? Nope."

"Always nice to see you, Chief, even if it is after the fact."

He gave me a gentle smile and grabbed my hand. "Seriously, Mackenzie, don't take any chances here, okay? Promise? We don't know who we can really trust at this point."

His tone—protective, fatherly—unsettled me a little. I cleared my throat and swallowed hard. "Sure, Chief. Promise."

CHAPTER TWENTY-SIX

T HE CHIEF SAT AT the end of the convent dinner table Monday night, opposite Sister Celeste Marie. She addressed the
group. "Sisters, this is Father Percival. He'll be with us for a few
days. Staying in the rectory while Father John is away."

After a round of introductions, he and Mother Angeline,
who was seated closest to him, started chatting. I tried not
to stare, but I've never known anyone as old as she. Let's be
honest—there aren't a lot of centenarians hanging around other
than in care facilities. Her white hair was in a perfect French
braid, and her skin glowed translucent under the dining room
lights. In her floor-length plain white habit, she looked, well,
beautiful. The picture of peace. Angelic.

When there was a lull in the table conversation, Sister Rosemary announced, "Archie came to the food pantry today."

My ears perked up. I resisted the urge to go all detective-y,
ask where I could find him, leave the table and track him down.
I took a deep breath and tuned in.

Bernadette said, "I'm glad to hear that. The poor man needs to eat."

Rosemary said, "I'd seen Harriet and Skip at the pantry this week, but not Archie. I was worried. He's usually at the pantry every day. Rare for him to be away so long."

I asked, "Did someone say he has a mental illness?"

Sister-Nurse Bernadette said, "Likely paranoid schizophrenia."

Rosemary turned to me. "He's not always in this world. Occasionally he will make perfect sense and you think you're having a conversation. The next minute, he's talking and making no sense at all."

I wanted to meet the guy, talk to him about Sister Mary Agnes. Maybe he was in the bell tower that night, saw something, heard something. Maybe I could catch him in one of those lucid moments. "Where is the food pantry?"

Rosemary said, "In the back of the cafeteria kitchen. Since we stopped offering hot lunches, we just use the kitchen occasionally now. We have a chicken dinner fundraiser and a pancake breakfast every year. But in between, we use the big pantry back there for donated food. We open it to the public for that hour, noon until one, Monday through Friday. When we open the door, there is often a line waiting. Families, singles, older folks."

"Where does the food come from?"

"The students hold a food drive every fall and spring as part of their community service requirements. And local businesses donate as well. We sometimes have so much, we don't have room for it all. We pray, and the Lord provides beyond all that we can ask or imagine," Rosemary said with a smile.

I wondered what it would be like to have that kind of faith.

After dinner, I went to my room for the hour of "quiet contemplation." According to the schedule, this included "examination of conscience." I found instructions online. "Recall your sins, be sorry, confess to the priest, do your penance."

That stopped me. No way was I confessing anything to the fake-priest-chief. And since I'm not even Catholic, did I need to confess at all? Gram would probably say yes.

The instructions went on to list examples of the seven deadly sins I'd found earlier in my research. Under sin of pride, had I been critical of others? *Uh, who hasn't?*

Had I been overly concerned about what others think of me and allowed that to direct my actions? My thoughts about Bo Peep—Hillary Sharp—at Spider's party came to mind. *Yep.*

Under lust, had I had impure thoughts? *Nick? Vince? Guilty as charged.*

Anger? Harboring resentments and grudges? *Hello, Sheena.*

Covetousness? *Oh, there's a Ten Commandments word.* Did that apply to my longing to leave the broom closet and possess "my" office? *Oh yeah.*

Envy? Comparing myself to others, wanting to have what they have? *Yes, yes, yes.* The green-eyed monster was alive and well.

Under the sin of sloth, one question jumped out: "Have I trusted God, especially in times of difficulty?" I couldn't say that I had. I tend to be independent and self-reliant. Is that so wrong? *Doesn't God have enough to do without me begging for help?*

Last on the list was gluttony. *If this applies to my addiction to sugar and drinking too much, then send me to the gallows.*

I sat back against the headboard. *Dang. We deserve to go straight to hell, do not pass GO, do not collect $200.*

I closed my eyes, not praying exactly, but hoping. Hoping that whoever or whatever God is, he-she-it might be willing to cut me some slack.

I went to the bathroom just after two a.m. Crossing the hall back to my room, I heard a noise from Mother Angeline's room, went to her door, rapped, and opened it. "Mother Angeline? Are you okay?"

Her bedside lamp was on. "Dreams," she said. "Bad dreams."

I went to her bedside and took her hand. "You're safe now. Everything is fine," I said.

She grabbed my hand, looked at me as if she could see something I could not. "Be careful, Mary Agnes. Promise me you'll be careful."

I was tempted again to correct her but didn't. "I will, Mother. But why do I need to be careful?"

She squeezed my hand with another piercing look. "Bad things are coming," she said. "Bad things are coming."

I said again, "I'll be careful."

She held on another moment, then said, "Good. Good." She released my hand and turned onto her side, closing her eyes.

I tucked her covers around her shoulders, turned off her lamp, and left.

Mother Angeline thought I was Mary Agnes, and she'd had a bad dream. The "bad things" were the stuff of nightmares, not reality. And her warning to me, just part of her confusion.

Rational Me offered assurance. *Not reality, just a bad dream. Just confusion, not reality.*

But then there was the way she looked at me. As if seeing something I couldn't see, knowing something I didn't know.

I tossed and turned the rest of the night.

CHAPTER TWENTY-SEVEN

A T MASS ON TUESDAY morning, the sun streamed through the stained-glass windows on the east side of the sanctuary. Dust motes floated through the rainbow of light.

My class and I sat midway back from the altar. The priest was not Father Percival, thank goodness, but Father Joseph from the neighboring parish.

I stared at an image of Jesus in the stained glass. He was surrounded by children. A metal plate beneath the window said it was donated to Holy Assumption church in 1976 by the Randolph family. I knew the name. Randolph Development Corporation owns a lot of commercial real estate in the area—the mini-mall on the south side, the River View motel on River Street, the building where Tansy rents her studio space, and the block where Lou's Vintage is.

The window depicted Christ seated on a large rock, a child on his lap and other children standing around him. I felt a sense of kindness in his eyes, patience with those children. The window exuded a sense of warmth even though it was all glass and lead.

I thought about the times at Gram's house when the whole clan is together. Greg's three kids and my sister Deanne's four. Wild times. Kids racing through the Victorian, lots of laughter and pure, unadulterated joy as they play, chasing each other, hiding from each other. Squeals of delight getting "caught." Gram, smiling through it all.

I wondered about the children in the window. Were they happy? Did they run and play and squeal with delight?

Later that morning, just before lunch, Sister Celeste Marie came into my classroom as the last student left. She closed the door and came to my desk. "Any progress to report?"

I had nothing. No answers, only questions. I told her I had nothing concrete—the truth—and then I lied and said, "I have several leads I'm working on."

She seemed okay with that and turned to leave.

"Sister, I noticed that beautiful window—Jesus and the children—during Mass. So different from the rest of the windows. Can you tell me about it?"

She sighed. "Yes, Ellie Randolph's parents donated the window in their daughter's memory after she died. They were devastated, naturally. We all were." She must have assumed I had no further questions and turned again to leave.

"How tragic. Was she ill, Reverend Mother?"

She stopped, hand on the doorknob, stood for a moment, then turned to face me. "It was long ago, just after I came to Holy Assumption. As I recall, she'd been depressed and simply decided she didn't want to go on. After her death, the family asked that a window be placed in the church in her memory."

I wondered if the girl had jumped from the bell tower, taken pills, or hanged herself in the shower. The investigator in me has an insatiable curiosity about such things and couldn't resist asking. "How did she die?"

Mother Superior glared. "What does that matter now? The poor child committed a mortal sin! It has nothing to do with your investigation. You have more current events to focus on." With that, she turned and marched out of the room.

Yes, Reverend Mother. Of course, Reverend Mother. Obsequious Me obeys authority.

CHAPTER TWENTY-EIGHT

I OFFERED TO HELP WITH the food pantry on Tuesday, hoping I'd get lucky and see the homeless folks I wanted to find. Sister Petronilla and I had served several couples when a single man, disheveled and dirty, came to the door. Petronilla greeted him. "Hello, Archie. Nice to see you today."

He looked at the ground as she handed him a lunch bag with a sandwich, carrot sticks, and an apple. He mumbled a thank you and started off toward the alley. I wanted to talk with him, so I thought fast.

"He forgot this," I said, grabbing a soda from the refrigerator. I hurried outside and caught up with him behind the church.

"Archie? I'm Sister Michelle. I'd like to speak with you a moment."

He turned and stared at me.

"Do you know where I can find Harriet? Or Skip?"

Blank stare.

"Archie, did you see Sister Mary Agnes in the bell tower? Did you see her fall? Last Saturday night?"

He crinkled his brow. What do the days of the week mean to a man on the streets? One day, one night, just like the rest. He looked up at the sky. "Gordon," he said.

"Gordon? Who is Gordon? Was Gordon at the bell tower?"

He said, "Comet. Eclipse. Jupiter." In the next moment, he was shambling down the alley.

I went back inside the school kitchen. I told Sister Petronilla what he'd said.

She said with a sad smile, "He's here and then he's not. You never know what he's talking about. Planets? Eclipses? That's Archie."

My chat with Archie yielded nothing of value. I had an hour free, and I hoped a visit to the Randolphs might give me more.

The Randolphs live just outside Three Rivers, in an area of rolling hills, vast lawns, and horses. I parked Cricket on the circular driveway in front of the house. I didn't call ahead, just hoped someone would be home.

A maid answered the bell and showed me into the library. Mrs. Randolph entered a few minutes later, dressed in tennis whites.

"Good afternoon, Sister. I don't believe we've met." We shook hands.

I explained that I was just temporarily at Holy Assumption but wanted to meet the people who donated the beautiful stained-glass window in the sanctuary. I lied and said that my family's home church needed to repair a window, and I'd said I would find out who did this one.

"We commissioned an artist in Chicago. That was years ago. I doubt that he's still in business."

"It was such a generous donation. And a beautiful window."

"Yes, we did that in memory of our daughter. She died, tragically."

"Oh, I'm so sorry." I needed to tread delicately. I waited. *Let them fill the silence.*

After a moment, Mrs. Randolph went on. "She was a student, back when Holy Assumption was a college. Such a happy girl. So full of life."

"Must have been a terrible shock for you," I said. I waited again.

"They told us that our daughter was depressed. I can't imagine why. She had everything she could ever want in this life. But people do change, especially when they go off to college. It was her first year at Holy Assumption, and she'd been so excited about "going away," even though it was only to live in the dormitory."

"No indication from her that she was depressed?" I hoped I wasn't being too nosy, arousing her suspicion. On the contrary, she seemed eager to talk.

"No indication, except for a phone call shortly before she died. She talked to my husband; told him she didn't want us to be disappointed in her. That's what she said. 'I don't want you and Mother to be disappointed in me.'"

"Any idea what she meant by that?"

"None whatsoever. Ellie was a happy girl, so bright. I can't imagine any way that she could have ever disappointed us."

CHAPTER TWENTY-NINE

WAS QUIETLY CONTEMPLATING MY conversation with Mrs. Randolph after dinner on Tuesday when my phone buzzed. A text from Heather Sullivan:

Donatellos NOW

All caps. Yelling for help. I shot down the back stairs and out to Cricket. Promising to be Heather's backup before I knew the convent schedule wasn't the smartest idea. I might have had a huge conflict when she texted, but the timing happened to be perfect. Lucky.

I imagined Petronilla saying, "We don't believe in luck. God is in control." Whatever. Luck or God—the timing was perfect.

I sped to Donatello's, parked on the street, and ran inside, scanning the bar and then the dining room. No Heather. Other diners looked surprised as I ran through the dining room toward the exit in the back. *Running nun, veil flying. Not quite like Sally Field.*

I hit the back parking lot, and there she was.

And there he was. Big and burly. And angry.

He had her from behind, squeezing her arms against her sides with a hand clamped over her mouth. He was shouting some very uncomplimentary things about Heather's femininity and parentage. She flailed, helpless.

I ran toward them, screaming.

He looked up, surprised, then gave a nasty laugh. "What the hell? A nun? What are you going to—"

I yelled, "That's Sister Impressive Badass to you, jerk!" I ran behind him and jumped on his back.

He couldn't handle us both. He let go of Heather, and she took a knee, gasping for breath.

He grabbed the sleeve of Mary Agnes's sweater and yanked hard. The frayed cuff ripped.

I yelled, "Oooh, Mother Superior is gonna be mad at you!"

He must have been Catholic because those words froze him. "Huh?"

Heather got up, whirled around and kneed him in the groin. He gave a strangled sound and doubled over. I held on to his neck as his knees hit the pavement.

He shifted hard to the right, and I fell off him. My right knee—and Gram's pantyhose—ground into the asphalt. "Now my grandma's gonna be mad!" *Pulling out the big guns.*

He was on all fours, trying to recover from Heather's knee to his nether region.

I jumped up and then came down hard, throwing my full weight onto his back.

He flattened onto the parking lot. He spewed more lies about the both of us as Heather got his hands cuffed behind him.

With one stiletto on the back of his neck, she yelled, "You have the right to remain silent—"

I hollered, "And I suggest you do!"

I got up and called 9-1-1. Just as Heather finished her Miranda spiel, sirens sounded in the distance.

I gave a statement at the scene, and the other cops left. Heather hung back.

I asked, "So, what happened with Mr. Wonderful?"

Heather gave a sneer. "You mean, Mr. Wonder-What-I-Was-Thinking? What an ass. So full of himself. We finished dinner and as we were leaving, he, um, requested that I, uh, perform certain—"

I held up a hand. "Got it. He expected to hook up."

"Yeah. In his car. Real classy. When I declined, he got a little, um, . . ." She snickered. "Huffy."

I smiled. "Huffy? Yeah, he was definitely huffy when I got here."

She looked at the pavement and gave her head a shake. "I can't believe I let him get the drop on me like that. His, uh, expectations threw me, I guess. I shouldn't have been surprised, considering the level of sleaze in the online dating world. But I was hoping for better." She gave a sigh.

We're all hoping for better, Lonely Me whispered. "You okay now?"

She brushed dirt off her sleeve. "No damage done, except to my pride." She reached out and grabbed my arm. "Thanks for showing up. I owe you big." She chuckled. "'Sister Impressive Badass'? Seriously?"

I laughed. "At your service, Detective Sullivan. Anytime."

She headed home and I drove Cricket back to the convent. I tiptoed in through the back door into the kitchen, just as Mrs. Jensen emerged from the butler's pantry.

She said, "Oh, it's you. I was just about to lock the door for the night."

"I'm sorry, Mrs. Jensen. I had an errand to run. Just going up to bed now."

"It's evening prayer time," she said, with a look that said she didn't think it her job to remind sisters when it was time to pray. She gave me the once-over, frowning.

I looked down. The right knee of Gram's pantyhose was shredded. Blood had coagulated on my knee. My blouse was half untucked and dirty. A thick black streak from the asphalt ran across the side of my skirt. No doubt my face was filthy and my hair a mess. I felt the top of my head. I'd lost my veil.

Mrs. Jensen scowled, probably wondering what the heck kind of a nun I was. She pointed at my sleeve. "I can stitch that up for you."

I looked down at the long tear in the cuff of the sweater. "No need. I'll take care of it." I thought I heard her mutter something like "suit yourself" as she walked away.

Later, there was a soft rap on my bedroom door. I opened it. Mrs. Jensen was there with a bottle of Bactine antiseptic spray. *No sting. No tears.*

"You'll need this for your knee." She handed me the antiseptic and a handful of Band-Aids and, without another word, left.

CHAPTER THIRTY

'D TAKEN A SHOWER and picked the gravel out of my scraped knee. I applied the antiseptic and bandages. Adrenaline was high, and I couldn't get to sleep.

My cell buzzed. A text from Vince.

> Sittin at Tap thinking about you.

Drunk Vince. A minute later, another text:

> Srsly thinking about you. Get together?

Now what girl doesn't love an elegant invitation like that one. I texted back:

> U R drunk. No thx.

My cell vibrated in my hand. Vince calling. I know I should ignore drunk Vince, but I answered.

He said, "You're right. I'm drunk, Banana Belly." His nickname for me back in my middle school days, a riff on Annabelle, my middle name.

"Don't call me that, Vincent."

"Okay, sorry. But you know this is when my real feelings come out, Banana—uh, Mackenzie."

"Your *real* feelings, Vince? If they were your real feelings, you'd be feeling them sober."

"I do! I do feel them sober, but I just can't talk about them sober."

Now, Vince isn't the first person to have this issue. I myself have trouble talking about feelings, so I can totally relate. So I said, "Okay, Vince, let's assume you have these feelings, and since you are drunk at the moment, tell me what they are."

He paused. "Aw, geez, Mackenzie. I don't know. I'm just nuts about you. That's all. I, uh, I want you."

"You didn't want me last Saturday night."

"Huh?" He went silent. "Oh yeah. That. Sorry. But I do want you."

"You want me for what exactly?"

He chuckled. "You know. Stuff."

"What kind of stuff, Vince?" *Geez, this is like pulling teeth,* Snarky said.

"You know what I'm talking about. Don't pretend you don't."

Snarky hissed. *Go ahead and ask him. Do you like me? Or do you like me like me?*

Of course, I knew exactly what kind of stuff Vince was talking about, and listening to him and acknowledging that I knew what he meant caused a wave of heat to race up from my toes to my chinny-chin-chin. I cleared my throat.

His voice soft, he said, "You want me too. I know you do."

He was right. The heat rose to my cheeks. "Uh, Vince, this is the kind of discussion we should have in person—" Before I could finish that sentence, he jumped on it.

"I'll be right there!"

"Wait!"

"No, no. Don't say wait!"

"No, Vince. Wait. I'm not home. I'm at the convent. Remember?"

Silence. He chuckled as the light dawned. "Oh yeah. That's right. You joined the convent. Bummer."

"I didn't *join* the convent. I'm working here this week. Undercover. Remember?"

More silence, then, "Yeah. Right. I remember. Okay. I gotta go."

"Please don't drive, Vince. Let the bar call HomeSafe for you, okay?" Old Town Tap is one of several bars in Three Rivers that takes part in the program that provides a safe ride home— no questions asked. "Vince, go home and sleep. We can talk later, after I finish up here. Next weekend maybe."

A decidedly disappointed Vince said, "Damn it. I should've just shown up at your place."

"No, Vince, bad idea because I'm not at my place. And besides that, I'd be responsible for getting you home, and I don't do that kind of thing. Not for anyone. Not anymore." I'd spent enough time in the codependent crazies taking care of my late ex-husband Billy and his out-of-control drinking.

Of course, back then I wasn't much better. I'd had too much to drink on too many occasions to count. But I was better now. Only drinking with friends, no longer every day. Well, sometimes home alone. But only wine. Because everyone knows that if you just drink wine, you can't have a problem.

I used my no-nonsense, newfound teacher voice and said, "Vince, get a ride and go home. Understand?"

A pause, then Vince mumbled, "Okay."

"You promise?"

"Yeah, yeah, I promise," he said and disconnected.

I plugged my cell phone into the charger, put it on Do Not Disturb, and tucked it under the table next to the bed. The wind howled outside, rattling the window. I thought of drunk Vince out in the night air. He'd been absolutely right about me, that I wanted to be with him, the same way he wanted to be with me. Stuff. Hot stuff.

Sin of lust, no question.

Sister Michelle Columbo, how do you plead?

Guilty, your honor.

Sister Michelle Columbo, you are guilty as charged.

CHAPTER THIRTY-ONE

THE NEXT MORNING, SISTER Celeste Marie pulled me aside and hissed in my ear. "Where were you? We missed you at evening prayer."

Evidently, Mrs. Jensen hadn't told her about the mess I was in last night. "I had an errand to run that couldn't wait."

She raised an eyebrow. "If you plan to fit in here, you must adhere to our traditions. You'll raise suspicion otherwise. The sisters wondered where you were last night, and I had no explanation. Next time, keep me informed."

Duly noted. "Yes, ma'am." I resisted saluting.

My fitness tracker vibrated on my wrist during the last half of my 11:00 a.m. class. I glanced at it. Text from Vince.

Need to talk

Not this again. How many times can a person's personal life disrupt her professional life? I'm trying to do my job here, people! A few seconds later, another Vince text popped up:

> Need you. Kenny is dead

Kenny was a firefighter and good friends with Vince and my brother Greg. He'd been having a rough time since his divorce last year. I gave a sigh. What can a friend do? Checking to be sure the students were involved in their discussion groups, I took out my phone and surreptitiously texted Vince:

> Rawley Park 12:15

At ten after twelve, I parked Cricket and waited for Vince. Sunlight sparkled across the Wolf River, beyond the bare trees. A cool breeze created swirls in the carpet of yellow and brown leaves on the ground, a mix of oak and maple. They'd soon be covered in snow, but not today.

Vince pulled in next to me in his Silverado and got into Cricket's passenger seat. His eyes were puffy and his hair a mess. "You look like hell, Vince," I said. "What happened to Kenny?"

He rubbed his hands over his face, then ran a hand through his hair. He swallowed hard, looking out the passenger window. "Offed himself this morning."

I knew from brother Greg that Vince and Kenny had been at a house fire the previous week. A five-year-old boy had died.

Vince said, his voice flat, "It was that fire. Kenny found the boy under a bed. Not breathing. Carried him out of the house, tried to revive him." Vince stared out the front windshield, seeing it all again, no doubt.

He turned to me. "I told Kenny it was too late, but he kept saying, 'Come on, come on,' to the kid, even though he was obviously gone. I'll never forget Kenny's face. Wildness in his eyes, frantic. He shoved me away."

He took a deep breath. "Kenny was a mess since that night. And then this morning, he did it. He texted me right before. Just said, 'I'm done.' I thought maybe he was resigning from the department. So I went to his place. He lived alone after his wife divorced him last year, you know?"

I nodded. "So, you went to his place—?"

Vince said nothing for a long moment, then gave his head a shake. "Yeah, yeah, I got there, and he was—" He sucked in a breath. "He was gone. Damn it, Mackenzie! Hanging in his garage. Oh, Jesus . . ."

Vince shook his head as tears streamed. What is it about a big tough guy breaking down like that? My heart broke for him, for Kenny and for the little boy. I reached to hold Vince. He leaned into me over the center console of the car. I remembered how he'd held me after my apartment fire, calming me, reassuring me. Time to return the favor. "How awful, Vince. I'm so, so sorry. So sorry."

We sat like that, Vince crying quietly, me holding him for several minutes. He finally sat up, wiped his palms across his face. He looked at me. "You must think I'm a real wuss."

"Not at all. You're human. That was awful for you."

"Jesus, Mack, we deal with that kind of thing all the time. We're trained to handle shit like that."

"Things like a good friend killing himself? How often does that happen?"

He went silent, staring out the front windshield. His voice got soft. "I keep seeing the kid. The way Kenny tried to bring him back. And then Kenny hanging there in the garage." He took a deep breath and looked at me, gave a shrug. "But, hey, all part of the job, right?"

I knew from Greg that the fire chief had been working to provide support for the team, but changes happen slowly. "Does the department have anyone you can talk to, Vince?"

"Ha! Like a shrink, you mean? Not a chance. I can figure this out." He gave me a smile and winked. "Maybe you can be my shrink, make me feel better."

I shook my head. "Sorry, dude. Not my job. There are professionals for that kind of thing."

"Yeah," he said. "The department hired Angela something. Or I could hire another kind of professional. Hope she's as hot as you are."

"I'm not talking about hookers! Dr. Angela is great."

Vince shook his head. "Not a chance. I'm not spilling my guts to a stranger. And what's she going to tell me? Nothing I don't already know. 'Feel it, let it go, and get back to work.' That's what they tell us to do."

His voice rose as his mood shifted. He glared at me as he opened the car door. "You know what? I came to you for support, and now you're telling me to see some quack. Screw that! Thanks for nothing!" He got out of Cricket and stomped toward his car.

I jumped out and ran after him. Grabbed his arm. He whirled to face me, stared a moment, then grabbed me and kissed me. I kissed him back. Whether he's sad or happy, drunk or sober, Vince is nice to kiss.

I heard giggling behind me. I turned, and there stood Lucy Lindstrom with two other girls. Her posse. On their lunch break. Lucy had her cell phone pointed at me.

Lucy sing-songed, "Ooh, Sister! Some nun you are!" The three of them laughed and walked away. "Have fun, Sister!" Lucy called over her shoulder.

Damn it! Anxious Me freaked out. *What are they going to say at school? Ohmigod, we've blown the whole case.*

Snarky piled on. *Nice going, Sherlock! The chief is going to be so pissed!*

Vince let me go and looked at me as if noticing how I was dressed for the first time. "Sister? You really *are* at the convent?"

"What? You thought I just made that up?"

"Wow. Never kissed a nun before." He laughed, a long, deep laugh. Sounding like the old Vince, he said, "Your cover is blown now. You know that, right? You'll be the hot gossip by tomorrow. Hell, they probably snapped a picture of us kissing and it's all over social media already."

"Ugh! Not the fifteen minutes of fame I was hoping for. I'd better get back to the convent."

Vince smiled. "Thanks for meeting me. I just needed someone to talk to. It helped. Really. Thanks." He gave me a quick hug and drove off.

I sat in Cricket for a few minutes, trying to think of what to do next. I didn't want to call the chief. I didn't want to hear his scolding for being so stupid.

And I sure as heck didn't want to have to tell Mother Superior that one of her charges was caught *in flagrante.*

Not sure which reaction I feared more, I started the car.

CHAPTER THIRTY-TWO

LATER THAT AFTERNOON, I was alone in the classroom, looking over the lesson plan for the next day. We'd be covering the female reproductive system.

I heard an "ahem" and looked up at Lucy Lindstrom, smirking at me. "So, Sister, who was that man you were kissing?"

"How is that any of your business?"

She leaned forward, supporting herself with her hands on my desk. "Oh, I'm *making* it my business. And I might just make it *every*one's business."

"Meaning?"

She stood up. "Meaning, I took a picture of you and that man." She waited.

"So? Not against the law to kiss people."

"So, if you don't give me what I want, I'm going to send it out to the world. I'm sure Reverend Mother will be very interested in it."

Fiendish little blackmailer. Brat. I leaned back. "What is it you want?"

"I want an A in this class. And I want you to write a recommendation for me for college."

I knew from the class records that Lucy hovered at a C-minus. "My grades suck, and my parents are pissed."

"Watch your mouth!" I slapped my palm on the desk.

She gave a snort and took a step back. "You're a fine one to talk."

I took a breath, as if I were actually thinking about her request. Calmly, I said, "Sorry, kid. I can't do it. It's dishonest."

She got huffy. "Seriously? You're worried about fudging a grade, when you—a nun!—and that guy are probably—" She dropped an F-bomb. "How *honest* is *that*? You all preach about chastity! What an effing joke!"

"Don't use that language with me, young lady." Saying that made me feel ancient. I softened. "Look, Lucy, what you saw isn't what you think."

She raised a brow. "Meaning what?"

"Things aren't always what you think they are."

She shrugged. "Still don't get your meaning."

"You'll have to trust me. Someday you'll understand. Meanwhile, I can't change your grade. That's up to you."

She gathered herself, shoulders back. "Fine, then! I'm going to post the picture on my socials, and you can kiss your sweet little nun life goodbye."

I scoffed. "Not quite how it works, Lucy, but nice try. Go ahead." I lied. "I've already told Reverend Mother about what happened, and she won't be pleased to hear you're trying to blackmail me."

She curled her lip and sneered at me. "Whatever. We'll just see what happens, won't we!"

"I guess we will." I stood and gave her my sternest look. "Now, if you have nothing more to say, I have lessons to prepare."

She glared at me and stomped out of the room.

I sat at the desk, shaking, willing my heart to slow and my body to calm. I didn't care a whit about my "reputation" as a nun. It was all fake anyway. What I did care about was the investigation, and having Lucy blow my cover might derail everything. I'd just started to gain the trust of the community. I couldn't risk ruining that.

I knew what I had to do. I ran out of the classroom. Lucy was at the end of the hall, ready to turn the corner.

"Lucy! Come back!"

She came to me.

"I've reconsidered," I said. "You're right. I don't want this to get out. I will change your grade for you."

She gave a smug smile. "I've reconsidered too. It's going to cost more than just a better grade."

"What do you have in mind?"

She shrugged. "Not sure yet. But I'll let you know."

"Will you delete the photo?" Worth a shot.

She laughed. "Not a chance. It's my insurance." As she turned away, she said, "I'll be in touch."

Snarky hated Lucy Lindstrom. *The little brat!* Rational Me knew that I was wise to buy more time to complete the investigation. More time to maintain my cover.

Badass Me agreed. *But once this sucker is done, watch out, you little b—!*

Lucy bumped into the chief—uh, Father Percival—as she left. "Sorry, Father," she said, head down as she started to run down the hall.

"Not a problem," he said after her.

The chief closed the door, and I explained what had happened at the park. He was not pleased. He had several words for me that you wouldn't expect from a priest. Not that I blamed him. This was my screw-up, plain and simple, and I had to make it right.

I told him what Lucy wanted.

He fumed. "She's blackmailing you? What a little—"

I held up a hand. "It's survival at that age. Her parents are on her case. She's just doing what she thinks she has to do." I remembered my own adolescent angst, the drama of teenage romance, the pressure for getting grades, choosing a college. "She's desperate." *Desperate enough to kill? Doubtful.* "How desperate would she have to be to blackmail a nun?"

He gave a shrug. "Well, since you aren't a real nun, it doesn't matter, does it? We just need to maintain our cover until we finish this investigation."

I filled him in on what I'd found so far, which was a whole lot of nothing. I had a study hall to monitor, so we left my classroom.

CHAPTER THIRTY-THREE

NICK TEXTED ON WEDNESDAY evening, during quiet time after dinner. He'd come back from his family trip and wanted to see me. *People, please!* I told him I'd meet him on the corner down the street from the church. The setting sun cast a warm glow over the neighborhood as I walked toward his Land Rover.

I got in, expecting dimples. I got a frown.

Before I could ask how his trip had been, or if his grandfather had had a nice birthday, Nick opened with, "I didn't want to have this conversation over text."

Uh-oh.

He said, "I heard—not that I put much store in gossip—but I heard that you and some other guy were making out at the Tap's Halloween party last Saturday."

"Who told you that?"

"Does it matter? Is it true?"

Ugh. Someone—everyone—had seen Drunk Morticia, going at it hot and heavy with Jack Sparrow. On the dance floor.

In the booth. Right in front of God and everybody. I cringed, imagining what I must have looked like.

"I was pretty drunk, Nick. Very drunk. You know how it is." Actually, I knew that Nick didn't know how it is to get drunk and act stupid in public. He didn't do that kind of thing. A beer once in a while, but that was it. Brave, clean, and reverent Nick. Boy Scout.

He got quiet. Very quiet. When he spoke, there was no hint of anger. His voice was soft, full of kindness, empathy, and all the other wonderful qualities he has. "You and I don't have any kind of commitment, I know, but I thought, well, I mean I hoped that we were heading somewhere in that direction. But if that's not the case, if you want to be with somebody else—and obviously you do—just tell me. If you don't want to be with me, please just tell me so we can both move on."

Nick was asking for clarification. Maybe for commitment. He was ready to commit. Don't we all think these days that the guys of our generation are afraid of commitment? Truth be told, it seems many of them are. But here was Nick. Sweet, dimpled, adorable Nick. Trustworthy, dependable, reliable Nick. Ready to commit. Laying his heart out there.

My throat felt tight. My mouth went dry. I wanted to look at him, but I couldn't. I couldn't meet those soft, brown eyes. Bambi eyes. Couldn't look at the sweet, sincere face. I looked at the floor of the car instead.

"I, uh, I don't . . . I mean it wasn't . . ." I swallowed hard, then looked up. "Nick, I don't think I'm ready."

The team in my head went nuts.

Anxious: *Not ready? What are you waiting for? Here is this perfectly adorable guy ready to commit to you, and you say you're not ready. Idiot!*

Snarky: *He's only saying this because he saw that someone else wants you, that's all. Typical guy!*

Lonely Me: *Take the deal. Take the deal.*

Rational: *Everyone just calm down. Tell him you have to think about it.*

Nick said, "You drank a lot that night at Spider's party."

A wave of shame and regret hit me.

"And sounds like you drank a lot again the night after that at the Tap."

A second wave. I wanted him to stop talking about this. I said, "But, Nick—"

He held up a hand. "Just hear me out. I love you, Mackenzie, and I'm concerned." First time Nick had ever used the L-word. A warm wave covered the shame as he took both my hands in his. "Would you consider not drinking for a while, just to see how it feels?"

Since I don't have any *real* drinking problem, I said, "Of course! I can quit anytime." A quiet voice whispered, *You sure about that?*

Nick smiled. "Okay. And now what about us?"

I checked my tracker. Almost time to get back to the convent. "Can I have some time to think about this?"

Nick's face fell. "I don't know what good that will do, Mack. We've had plenty of time to think. More time for thinking isn't going to change anything." He met my eyes, serious. "It's yes or no at this point."

I felt tears welling, and my face got hot. "You're demanding an answer. Now? You just show up and demand an answer on the spot. That's not fair."

He shrugged. "Fair or not, I don't think it's complicated. You want me or you don't. Simple."

Yes or no? Yes or no? Yes or no?

If I didn't want Nick, did that mean I wanted Vince? I'd wanted them both, but now I wasn't sure I wanted either one of them. And I sure didn't like the idea of Nick demanding an answer. Right. Now.

Snarky huffed, *At least Vince would* never *accuse you of having a drinking problem!*

Rational Me wondered if that was a good thing.

Nick looked so sad, I wanted to grab him and tell him what he wanted to hear. But that would be dishonest. Just the old codependent me wanting to be sure everyone else is fine. That middle child curse I carry, wanting to make everybody happy. Putting up with the broom closet office. Saying yes when I really want to say no. Pretending I'm okay when I'm not. *No wonder we drink,* Anxious Me whispered.

Not saying what I really want, need, think, or feel to avoid upsetting anyone. Badass said, *We're not doing that anymore.*

I took a deep breath. "If you are demanding an answer, putting me on the spot, well, I guess the answer is no for now, but not forever."

He nodded. "Okay. Thanks for being honest. I gotta get going."

My cue to leave. I watched the Land Rover disappear around the corner, wanting to text him to make sure we were okay, that he wasn't angry with me. To ask him if he accepted the "not no forever," which almost definitely implied a "maybe yes in the future," but he was gone.

I pulled my cardigan closer against the night air and, as I walked back to the convent, I called Tansy. I told her about Vince and about Nick. "Do you think I drink too much?"

She gave a long pause. "Who am I to judge?"

"Tans, I trust you. We've been friends since middle school. You've always had my back. So, I'm asking you. Do you think I drink too much?"

She gave a sigh. "Well, sometimes you do get carried away, Mack, but heck, don't we all? The important question isn't what *I* think, but do *you* think you drink too much?"

Rational Me: *It will be fine. We'll just cut back. We can control this.*

Anxious Me felt a rise of panic. *Oh my God, stop before something awful happens!*

Badass weighed in. *It's not like we're driving drunk, getting in bar fights. Jesus, quit worrying about it!*

Tansy repeated the question. "Mack, what do *you* think?"

"I think I have a lot to think about."

I disconnected. The moon had risen behind the church, casting the bell tower's shadow on the sidewalk before me. I passed the Jensen house and thought I saw a curtain move in the front window. I felt a wave of apprehension. Had someone seen me on my cell phone? Or in Nick's car?

I shook it off and continued to the convent. Back in my room, I sat on the bed and googled "how to tell if you have a drinking problem." A quiz. *Aha! This will prove I'm right.*

The results after the quiz: "If you answered yes to between 8 and 20 questions, you most likely are a functional alcoholic."

I'd said yes to eight of them. Anxious Me was tempted to take the quiz over again to make sure that number was lower.

The next words were a punch in the gut. "You may feel like your alcohol use is completely under your control. Sadly, this is the lie that many functioning alcoholics believe."

I thought about how Drunk Me is Stupid Me and how she'd made a complete ass of herself with Vince that night. And the fallout from that was that Nick was hurt. And sad. And maybe heartbroken. And he deserved better than that.

And what was I thinking with Vince? Was I just using him to make myself feel sexy? Or wanted? Or what? Vince deserved better too. Like I said, Drunk Me is definitely Stupid Me.

I sat back against the headboard. That nagging voice inside asked, *Is it possible I really do have a problem?* I'd lost countless nights and weekends over my short life, having "fun" and "letting off steam." Usually wine, but like the night with Vince, sometimes harder stuff. I'd convinced myself I didn't have a problem because I don't drink every single day. But to be honest, the days I didn't have anything to drink were usually the days I was hungover from the night before.

I heard that nagging voice again: *How much more time do I have before awful things started to happen to me?*

I thought about my Aunt Fiona, my mother's youngest sister. She's a for-sure, legit alcoholic, which she jokes about. "I'm not an alcoholic. I only drink when I'm alone or with somebody."

Very funny, Fiona. Any time someone suggests she might have a problem, she laughs. "Lighten up, for Christ's sake. Who made you the booze police?"

So, in examining my own issue—if I even *have* an issue—I can honestly say I'm not like my aunt Fiona. I'm not *that* bad. Still, maybe it was time to consider letting an old habit go.

CHAPTER THIRTY-FOUR

COULDN'T THINK ABOUT NICK or any drinking problem I may or may not have for one more minute. I'd figure that out another day. For now, I had to get my mind back on the case.

I sat in the rocking chair, staring out into the darkness. What did I have? A big pile of nothing.

Most likely, Sister Mary Agnes got dizzy and fell accidentally. Blame the medication she took. Was anyone else in the bell tower? Maybe this Archie from the streets. He may have tracked in the mud Dutton had mentioned. But that didn't mean he had anything to do with her death.

There was Lucy, the angry student. Trying to blackmail me was one thing, but to murder for a grade? Fat chance.

What was that unforgivable whatever that Sister Mary Agnes felt compelled to confess? No clue.

I felt stuck. My variation of "What would Jesus do?" is "What would the chief do?" He'd already told me to keep thinking, keep digging. But where? I'd done online research of Holy Assumption's history. I'd dug as far and as deep as I could.

Online pictures showed the old dormitory—two stories of red brick, similar in color to the church and convent. I'd seen old yearbook pictures online as well, from the 1930s to the 60s. The pictures reflected the changes in women's fashion, from dresses like their mothers wore through the era of bobby socks, saddle shoes, and poodle skirts. Not a pair of jeans in sight.

I imagined them laughing together, studying together, sneaking out at night for fun, like Mrs. Sharp had said. That's what college girls do, right?

All that was long ago. What about here and now? I didn't know where else to go or what to do to resolve this case. Jesus and the chief weren't helping, so I went to the one reliable source in my life. I whispered to the window, "What would Gram do?"

I knew the answer instantly. She'd pray.

I've never been a praying person, other than following along during services at Our Savior's. I prayed as a ten-year-old, but my daddy didn't come back. And my grandfather, Papa Powell, still died despite my fervent child prayers. I learned early that prayer doesn't really work.

Maybe it was a combination of Gram's example and being at the convent, around all those women who actually believed in prayer. Whatever.

I checked the time and the schedule. Free time for the community. I headed to the labyrinth.

The space under the church was cool and silent. Insulated from the world, a sacred quiet permeated the air. This underground labyrinth must have served the sisters well all winter, when it was too cold to walk and pray outside. And in our summers, this would have provided a cool respite from heat and humidity.

For decades, religious sisters trod the stones beneath the church, hour after hour, praying for an end to wars, an end to poverty, the liberation of the imprisoned.

Praying for mercy. For redemption. For forgiveness.

I started on the outside ring. I walked the stone path, imagining the generations of walkers. Was this a penance for some? *Ten Hail Marys and six hours on the labyrinth?* Or was this a place to say the rosary or just commune with God in your own words?

I took Sister Mary Agnes's rosary from my pocket, feeling the smooth beads as I walked. *What are the words?* I'd researched online. Part of the rosary prayers included the "Our Father," as they called it here at Holy Assumption. At Gram's church, they called it the "Lord's Prayer."

I walked the stone path. With each step, I sensed I was leaving the past behind me, entering the future. Step by step by step.

Gram has long insisted she knows when God is speaking to her.

I'd ask her, "But *how* do you know?" I pleaded for more specifics just in case God ever decided to say something to me. I'd want to be ready.

Gram's answer? "You just know."

I listened, slowed my steps to listen more closely. I figured if God was ever going to speak to me personally, it would be in a place like this.

I heard nothing. Strained harder to hear. Nada. The only sound in the space was the occasional squeak of my shoes against the stone.

I was ready to give up when I sensed something. Not that I heard an audible voice. I felt something. A thought? A feeling?

An impulse? Hard to define. Was it divine guidance? Direction? Or was it my own intuition, kicking in with the meditative rhythm of my steps?

Whatever. I knew what I had to do. I headed back to the convent, ignored the invitation to join the game of Monopoly in the dining room, and went to my room, where I quietly formulated my next steps.

CHAPTER THIRTY-FIVE

I T WAS JUST AFTER eleven Wednesday night when I opened my bedroom door and listened. No sounds from any of the other rooms. I'd dressed again in my sweats and grabbed my TriMak flashlight before I tiptoed down the back stairs of the convent. Again.

This time, I headed to the blocked tunnel. Something was in one of those rooms in the tunnel, something important. I'd sensed that on the labyrinth.

I reached the tunnel and ducked past the barricade. Flashlight guiding my way, I reached the first of the three rooms. The door wasn't locked. I opened it and flashed the light around the space. Empty. Ditto for the second storeroom.

I reached the third door, the one closest to where the old dormitory had stood. This door was padlocked. *What's here that needs to be protected?*

I tugged on the lock, and it opened. Rational Me knew it opened because whoever closed it last obviously didn't close it tightly. Another part of me whispered, *Thanks, whoever.*

I closed the door behind me and swept the light around. A light switch next to the door proved useless. This room was empty, but another padlocked door was on the opposite side of the room. I crossed to it.

This padlock was locked. The wooden door seemed to give a little. I pushed again, harder. A little more give. I ran at the door, shoulder first, like you see in the movies. Bam! And ouch! The hasp of the padlock gave way, and the door swung open. Badass was thrilled. *Oh yeah.*

A chemical smell hit me first. Formaldehyde, maybe, if my memories of biology class served me. I found a light switch. Fluorescent lights overhead buzzed to life as I stepped inside.

A doctor's office table with stirrups stood in the middle of the room. A double metal sink on one wall, next to shelves holding glass jars and metal objects. Surgical instruments. All covered in dust. Cobwebbed. Long—decades maybe—unused.

What was it here for? Did the convent sisters have their own medical care here? Perhaps they'd been cloistered here in the past, and outsiders were forbidden.

A cabinet at the far side of the room. The top half had two shelves above a desktop surface with a drawer below. The shelves held old books. I read the titles.

Fractures and Dislocations. Intestinal Management. Women's Medical Problems. Surgical Guide to Amputations. Nervous System Anatomy.

I took a volume titled *Practical Gynecology* from the shelf. Opened the cover. "M. Phelps" was written inside. I turned to the copyright page. Published in 1956. I checked some of the others. All belonged to M. Phelps and were published in the 1940s and 50s. None were more current.

Sister Celeste Marie had mentioned the community availing itself of medical care as needed. Was that true decades ago? Perhaps medical issues were dealt with "in-house."

I opened the drawer under the desk. Miscellaneous items—a couple of handkerchiefs, pens, a pack of Camel cigarettes, and several matchbooks.

I picked up a small notebook, about five-by-seven inches, and riffled through it. Neat columns in a tight, precise handwriting indicated dates in the 1950s and early 60s, with times and initials only, no names.

DATE. TIME. PATIENT. ISSUE. PROCEDURE.

Some issues were obvious: colds, flu, minor cuts—the kind of stuff you go to urgent care for these days. Others were in a kind of shorthand. ST: Sore throat, maybe? UTI: Urinary tract infection. That one I had personal experience with.

Halfway down the first page, one entry caught my eye: Issue: PG. Gram used that instead of saying "pregnant."

Procedure: D&C

My stomach dropped. I knew what that meant. Abortion.

I looked at the other pages. A few other entries were the same, scattered among the mundane maladies.

I stood a moment, letting this information sink in. Who was this M. Phelps? Male or female? A doctor? A nurse? Working in the basement of a girls' college dormitory. A *Catholic* girls' college. Performing abortions.

We'd all heard horror stories about "back-alley abortionists" and women being maimed—butchered, really—bleeding to death, at worst, or rendered unable to have children.

I turned to the last notations, midway through the ledger. The last entry was dated May 15, 1966. Another "PG" and "D&C" for a patient with the initials E.R.

I stared, stunned. Ellie Randolph? Could it be?

Whoever M. Phelps was, he or she had stopped doing what they were doing in 1966. The year Ellie Randolph died and the college closed.

I needed to get out of this room and find the chief. As I turned to leave, I noticed one last cabinet on the wall near the door. I opened the doors. Two shelves. The lower shelf full of books.

Several small jars lined the upper shelf. The smell of formaldehyde was overpowering. I looked closer.

Tiny bodies. Little legs. Fragile faces.

Fetuses.

I closed the doors, turned away, ran across the room to the sink and promptly threw up.

When the spasms stopped, I bent from the waist, hands on my knees, taking deep breaths until my stomach settled.

I touched the ledger in my sweater pocket and felt the cool beads of Sister Mary Agnes's rosary. I prayed silently for the souls of the girls and the babies represented in this room. I couldn't imagine being in a situation that desperate.

I turned out the light and did my best to close the bashed-in door behind me. Evidence of my intrusion, but it couldn't be helped.

I crossed to the outer door and pulled. It didn't give. I pulled again, harder. I'd left the open padlock hanging in the hasp. It couldn't lock itself.

Someone obviously locked me in. My heart thumped as sweat formed on my upper lip.

I listened. Silence outside. Tried the door again and again. Why do we do that? *Didn't work, so I'll just keep doing the same thing over and over.* The definition of insanity, right?

Call the chief! That would have been a brilliant choice, but for the fact that my cell phone was currently plugged into the charger under Mary Agnes's bed. *Stupid!*

I didn't have any other options, so I started pounding on the door, yelling for help. *Ridiculous! Nobody will be around at this hour.*

After ten minutes of hollering and pounding, my voice was hoarse and my hands sore. Then, wonder of wonders, light from the hallway shone under the door. I heard a key in the padlock, and the door opened.

I flashed my light into Mr. Jensen's face as he aimed his at me.

His face a mix of surprise and concern, he said, "I was just makin' my midnight rounds, and I heard you calling. How in tarnation did you end up down here, Sister?"

I stepped quickly out of the room and pulled the door shut behind me. I didn't want him noticing how I'd broken into the second room.

As we walked out of the tunnel, I told him I'd been walking the labyrinth and got lost and hoped one of these doors would take me out of the tunnel. "This place is just so confusing. All these tunnels are like a maze!" Of course, that didn't explain how I ended up in a room that was padlocked from the outside, but I talked fast, doing my best nun imitation. "Praise to the Good Lord that you came along, Mr. Jensen! Please be kind enough to help me find my way back to the convent?"

He evidently bought my story. We chatted about the weather and the school carnival plans as he led me back through the tunnel, past the underground labyrinth, then up to the church vestibule. "I know the way from here, Mr. Jensen. Thank you so much."

He touched the brim of his ever-present canvas hat. "Good thing I came along when I did, Sister."

"Indeed, Mr. Jensen. Indeed," I said and headed to the steps to the convent tunnel.

Back in my room, I left Heather Sullivan a voicemail at a quarter to one. I figured she owed me a favor after I saved her from Sleazebag, Esquire in Donatello's parking lot.

"I need deep background on an M. Phelps." I spelled the last name. "A doctor, or maybe a nurse, practicing in this area in the 50s and 60s."

I texted the chief:

Need to talk.

Father Percival was no doubt sleeping peacefully while I was working in the middle of the night. Whatever.

I tried to sleep while images of what I'd seen in that room floated in and out. Bad things. Bad things.

CHAPTER THIRTY-SIX

AT TWENTY AFTER SIX on Thursday morning, I was dressed for the day. I checked my phone. Nothing from Heather, not that I expected anything from her so early. But the chief had texted back:

My car 6:30.

The sky was just beginning to lighten, but the sun wouldn't be up for another hour or so. I opened the window and inhaled deeply of the fresh, cold dawn, trying to chase away the memory of formaldehyde and death.

A chill gust of wind blasted through the room. I closed the window and turned to head down to the main floor chapel, to join the others for prayer and meditation before breakfast. I ignored Snarky as she whispered, *Well, well, well, aren't we just the perfect little nun?*

The picture of Jesus on the wall hung askew. Rational Me

assumed the gust of wind had moved it. What else could it have been? I don't believe in ghosts.

I took the frame off the wall to rehang it straight. The cardboard backing bulged. *Curious.* I took it to the bed, bent up the four little metal tabs, and removed the cardboard. Three envelopes were tucked behind the backing along with a folded piece of paper.

"Well, hello there." Each envelope held an index card with letters cut from magazines, like ransom notes. Each had the same single word:

SILENCE

Someone threatening Sister Mary Agnes before she died. Who? Why? I unfolded the piece of paper. A letter or a journal page, undated, torn from a spiral notebook. "Lord, forgive me," it began. A prayer, a letter to God, asking forgiveness. The content was vague. "I thought it was your will."

The end got a little more specific. "I did what she told me to do." Then, "I kept the secret. It was wrong, I know." And finally, "Now it's time for me to pay for my sin." It ended as it had begun. "Lord, forgive me."

I sat and looked at the cards and the letter, laid out on the bed. Three notes. Three threats. *From whom? Silence about what?* One confession. *Of what?* Maybe that unforgivable unknown whatever Sister Mary Agnes carried.

I reassembled the back of the picture and hung Jesus back on the wall. I tucked the index cards and letter into the envelope with the police report and the ledger from the basement room.

I got dressed, and as I headed into the hallway, Mother Angeline was coming from the bathroom. Since she'd been around since the beginning of time, I decided to ask her about the room in the dorm basement tunnel.

"May I talk with you, Mother?

She stared at me a moment. "Of course, dear."

I followed her back to her bedroom. She took a seat on the edge of the bed, and I sat in the small chair against the far wall. "I've seen something in the basement of the dormitory, and I have questions about it, Mother Angeline."

A twitch of her eyebrows told me she knew something, But she gave me a blank look.

"There were medical books there," I said.

No reaction but for a tightening around her mouth.

"A doctor's office?"

She stared past me to her bedroom window as she crossed her arms.

I asked, "Mother Angeline? Do you know anything about that?" I wanted to shake her to the present moment, interrogate her. She had to know something about what happened in that room. She was here back then. I wanted to demand to know what she knew about abortions in the basement of the Holy Assumption College for Women. The scandal that happened back there.

She started to rock slowly back and forth, hugging herself, singing words of a hymn I didn't recognize. "Mother of mercy . . . poor banished children . . . mother of mercy . . ."

Mother Angeline had left the building. I patted her shoulder. "It's okay, Mother. It's okay. No more questions." I left her rocking and singing.

I checked my fitness tracker. Time to meet the chief. It was a risk, meeting him behind the convent at such an early hour. I found Sister Celeste and told her I needed to talk with him.

Keeping you informed, as requested, ma'am! She excused me from prayer.

Father Percival was behind the wheel when I got to his car. He started it as soon as I buckled myself in.

"Where are we going?"

"Just driving around so we can talk without being noticed."

I told him I'd asked Heather for information on M. Phelps, whoever that was. I told him what else I'd found in the room, evidence of illegal abortions being performed, "in the basement of a *Catholic* girls' college!"

He wasn't as shocked as I expected him to be. "I've seen it all, Chickie. People pretending to be one thing when they're really another. Lousy families pretending they're just fine. Abusers on Saturday night showing up all clean and shiny for church on Sundays. Human nature, I guess, holding up a false front, an image that has nothing to do with reality."

"But *abortions*, Chief? Moral questions aside, it was illegal then."

"Back then, girls in trouble didn't have many options."

"Well, I was shocked. All those jars. I puked in the sink."

"We'll go back down there tonight, after everyone has gone to bed. I want to see for myself."

I told him about the notes and the letter I'd found behind the picture of Jesus. "Definitely someone threatening her, right? And she was going to confess something."

He said, "And someone didn't want that to happen."

"No question. But who? Mother Angeline knows something, but she can't say what it is." I told him about questioning her earlier. "I'll try her again later. Her memory might be better or worse, depending on the time of day." I'd experienced that coming and going of memory with Nathan.

We turned the corner onto Pike and Third to head back to the convent. A familiar figure was crossing the street. "Hey, that's Archie!" I pointed, and the chief pulled to the curb. I jumped out. "Archie! Archie!" I called and started trotting in his direction, hoping he'd be more coherent this time. I caught up to him.

"Remember me? Sister Michelle? From the food pantry."

He shook his head, mumbled something, and started to walk away.

I grabbed his sleeve and stopped his forward motion. He turned. I got closer to him. He met my eyes.

"Archie, it's very important. The other day, you said you saw someone at the church when the sister died. You said the name *Gordon*. Do you know Gordon's last name?"

A long shot. Archie looked at me, trying to focus.

I repeated, "Gordon?"

He shook his head and patted his chest with his palm. "No. Archie."

"Yes, I know you're Archie, but who is Gordon? Remember? He was at the church when Sister died. In the bell tower?"

He crinkled his face, shook his head, and pulled away from my grasp. He walked away muttering to himself.

I had a name. Maybe. Gordon something. Or something Gordon. Back at the chief's car, I told him what Archie had said. "So, who is this Gordon? Ring any bells, Chief?"

He shook his head. "Ask the sisters. Maybe one of them will know."

As we drove back to the convent, Heather texted a link to licensing and other information for Matthew Phelps, MD. I have to admit, I liked this more cooperative Heather, even if she was just being that way because she wanted that promotion.

I read aloud as the chief drove. "Phelps died of lung cancer in 1967 at the age of 59. Licensed in Wyoming. Army doctor 1943 to 1946, then worked at a hospital in Wyoming until 1952. Left there and worked at Saint Dominic's Hospital in Chicago until 1954. Then nothing. His medical license expired in 1958. No malpractice, no charges indicated."

The chief turned down the alley toward the convent.

I said, "How does a doctor from Wyoming end up, with no license, performing illegal procedures in the basement of a college dormitory in Three Rivers in the 1950s and 1960s?"

The chief said, "And who knew about it? Who among the current sisters was around back then?"

I said, "Mother Angeline was certainly there, but can she remember? Or will she tell what she knows? And Sister Celeste was there, and so was Mary Agnes. I'm pretty sure her unforgivable sin must have had something to do with what was happening in that basement."

"This doctor would have an assistant, wouldn't he?" the chief asked.

I nodded. "Sister Bernadette is actually a nurse. Maybe she was involved back then." I pictured the other sisters. "Petronilla, Prudence, Rosemary, and Doris aren't old enough to have been around then. At least I don't think so. Hard to be sure about their ages."

The chief pulled into a parking spot behind the convent. "And there are others who've died or moved on since then. Impossible to track them down."

I said, "Seems there was somebody in the bell tower the night she died. Gordon somebody? Or Archie himself? Or someone else?"

The chief said, "I did some digging, and the guy they call

Skip has been in county lockup for two weeks. And Harriet has been in the hospital."

Dead ends for them. I was grasping for anything at all. I said, "For all we know, it was Lucy Lindstrom."

"Who?"

"The blackmailer. Or maybe Sister Celeste herself. Or maybe this artist, Perry Cuthbert."

The chief said, "Ah, I remember him coming when I was in school. Always a big deal when he came to town. Geez, he's gotta be pushing ninety these days. How many more times is he going to make the trip?"

"This is his last year. He's got some health issues, Sister Petronilla told me."

"It's worth checking him out. Try to arrange a meeting with him."

"Yes, sir, Father-in-chief," I said.

"Don't be a smartass, Chickie," he said as we got out of the car. He was chuckling as we went inside for breakfast.

After breakfast—two hard-boiled eggs, an orange, and two slices of toasted raisin bread with lots of butter—I found Sister Celeste alone at her desk.

"Got a minute?"

She nodded. "If it's quick." She put the papers she'd been working on in a manila folder and put it in her desk drawer. "What is it, Sister Michelle?"

Leaning toward her and keeping my voice low, I told her about the index cards and the prayer Agnes had written out.

She paled as a hand went to her heart. "Are you saying that Mary Agnes got them too?"

I leaned away from her, my voice rising several decibels. "What do you mean—'too'?"

She looked up at the crucifix on the wall, then back at me. "I received a card like that two weeks before Mary Agnes died." She met my eyes. "Mine had that same word. SILENCE. Gave me a chill."

"You didn't mention this to the police?"

"Of course not. It was a private matter within the community. I had no idea it would have anything to do with Agnes's death. I had no idea she'd received notes as well. But now I realize there may be a connection."

Duh! Ya think? I swallowed hard. "Yes, Sister, there is no doubt a connection. Can you tell me what you think your card was referring to?"

She shook her head. "No, no. I can't say for certain. Anything I offer would be merely conjecture."

I pressed forward. "Conject away, please, Sister!"

She shook her head. 'No. No, I won't. I mustn't." She drew her lips into a tight line.

I said, "Sister Agnes's sister said that Agnes mentioned what she called 'an unforgivable sin.' Any idea what she was talking about? Because I think this letter and these cards are about that."

She looked down at her hands, folded in her lap. She closed her eyes. After several moments, she looked up, shaking her head.

I was sick of her stalling. "Sister Celeste, something happened here, back in the 1960s. And I found the room in the basement that was the, uh"—I chose my words carefully—"the doctor's office." I was absolutely sure that there was a connection, and I was equally sure Sister Celeste knew all about that connection. I said no more, just watched her face.

She went pale as her wimple and looked down at the desk. She cleared her throat, then said, "I can't say anything about that."

Can't say? Or won't say? Neither of those did *I* say.

Whatever the big scandal was, Sister Celeste wasn't about to tell me about it. I'd need to check other sources—Heather, the chief, the other sisters—to get the skinny. *Ooh, get the skinny. Very detective-y talk.*

She stood and pointed to the dining room. "It's time for class."

End of discussion. Yes, ma'am.

I know when I've been dismissed.

CHAPTER THIRTY-SEVEN

S CHOOL WAS OUT FOR the day. I met Sister Petronilla at the school gym to join the other sisters in preparing for the carnival the following day. She told me how important the Halloween Carnival was for Holy Assumption's fundraising. "We charge ten dollars at the door, twenty for a family. We have a silent auction going all evening. Last year, the big item was a fishing boat and motor. But this year's big-ticket item is extra special. Come and see."

She led me to a classroom across the hall from the gym. Sister Doris was draping a cloth over an easel.

Petronilla said, "Perry Cuthbert donated a painting for our auction. Sister Doris, may we see the painting, please?"

Doris removed the cloth with great reverence, as if she were unveiling the Mona Lisa. She stepped back.

Two angelic figures of delicate pale blue-gray, one smaller, one larger, floated on a backdrop of deep blue. They seemed almost transparent. In the lower right, a single drop of red.

We three stared at it for several long moments.

"Stunning, isn't it?" Petronilla whispered.

"Reminds me of a Chagall," Sister Doris said, her voice soft, reverent.

I remembered Marc Chagall from art history class in college. "Isn't he the one with the goat playing the violin in his paintings?"

Petronilla chuckled. "Yes. Don't you wonder what the goofy goat is about?"

Sister Doris frowned. "We make fun of that for which we have no appreciation." She looked at us over the rim of her glasses. "Or understanding."

Ouch. Stupid!

Doris pushed her glasses back in place. "Perry is influenced by Chagall, obviously, but he's given this piece a simplicity with clean lines and a limited color palette. And yet the figures are alive against the backdrop, as you can see. They float there and, when we gaze long enough, we sense a gentle movement between them, as if they are dancing together."

I squinted at the angel figures. Dancing? I couldn't see it. Snarky huffed again. *Dilettante!*

Sister Doris went on. "Hence the title of the piece—Ellie's Dance."

Ellie? "Does that refer to Ellie Randolph, the girl who died? The one whose family donated the Jesus window?"

Sister Doris nodded. "Yes."

Mental note: Dig.

Petronilla said, "It's beautiful. And we could reach our fundraising goal with this painting alone." She turned to me. "Perry has works in several New York galleries and even has a painting in the Museum of Modern Art. He's quite famous."

Again, I had no idea someone like that had come from our neck of the woods. "He was just here, wasn't he? I wish I could have met him."

"Oh, he's still in town and will be here tomorrow night to present the painting to the auction winner."

MUCH LATER, JUST AFTER MIDNIGHT THURSDAY night, I crept out of the convent and through the tunnel to the church basement again. The chief was waiting near the labyrinth for me. We headed to the room at the end of the dorm tunnel. The padlock was gone from the door. I pushed the door open, and we stepped inside. I played the beam of my flashlight around the room. The door to the second room stood open. I walked quickly into the back room and flipped the light switch. Nothing. Had the power been disconnected, or had those old fluorescents given up the ghost after my visit? We swept the room with our flashlight beams.

Empty.

Completely stripped. No desk. No doctor's office table. No books. No jars of dead babies. Nothing. Not a cobweb was left.

A strong odor of bleach hung in the room. "Someone scrubbed this place," the chief said.

I walked to the sink. No sign of my getting sick. The sink was sparkling clean. I leaned into it and sniffed. "Yep. Bleach. Somebody wanted whatever secret was here to stay a secret."

The only evidence that remained that any of it had even existed was the little ledger book, hidden temporarily between the mattress and box spring of Sister Mary Agnes's bed.

CHAPTER THIRTY-EIGHT

H ALLOWEEN HAD ARRIVED, AND the students were allowed
to dress in costume—within reason, of course. Following
that "your body is a temple" edict from the Bible. Encouraged
to dress like historical or fictional figures, one boy was Uncle
Sam, another was Robin Hood. Another was Colonel Sanders,
and Abraham Lincoln was in the mix as well. I saw two girls
dressed as nurses, and more than one Cinderella walked the
corridors.

It was lunch hour on Friday, and I needed food. The convent kitchen was the perfect place to rustle up some grub for
myself.

Ooh, rustle up some grub. Who are you? Hoss Cartwright?
Snarky has got to stop watching old Westerns on family-friendly
TV with Gram.

I came around the back porch of the convent and saw someone in a habit—the old-school black-and-white version—at the
back door, facing away from me. I thought it might be Sister
Celeste, but nobody was usually home during the lunch hour.

I said, "Excuse me, Sister. Can I help you with something?"

She stiffened. Without turning around, she said, "My key isn't working."

Now, I knew that was a big fat lie because the back door of the convent is only locked at night, after "lights out" at ten p.m. "That's not possible," I said, "because—"

She turned around. My jaw dropped. "Sheena? What are you doing here?"

Her eyes wide, she grabbed my arm and shook it, almost shouting, "Oh my God! I got so bored at that cabin! I don't know how you people here in the sticks think it's fun to stare at a lake and listen to loons all the damn day and night. Jesus Christ! I almost lost my mind!"

I looked around, hoping nobody heard her. "Stop cussing! Come with me." I grabbed her by the sleeve, pulled her off the porch. She followed me to Cricket. I opened the passenger door. "Get in!"

I got in the driver's side as she huffed. "Jesus, there's nobody around to hear me. What is your problem?"

I huffed back. "First of all, you are on religious turf here, so kindly stop swearing."

She sneered. "Oh? Like you don't?"

"Not here, I don't. Have a little respect! Now tell me what the hel—uh, heck you're doing here."

"It's that damn—sorry, *darn*—doodle. I couldn't stand him another minute. I had to get him back to Trip's house."

"I thought you loved Curly."

"Oh, he's cute, and he was fine when we were here in town. Trip insisted I take him to the cabin. 'For protection,' he said."

"Do you think those bad guys are still after you?" I still didn't know what had happened to make her a target.

She talked faster. "Yeah, those guys are not the type to forgive and forget. Short on smarts but long on grudges. Anyway, the dog wasn't any good for protecting me. At the lake, he barked at everything. I mean *every stinkin' thing.*"

"How annoying," I said, picturing being stuck in a small cabin with a big, floppy, barking dog. Of course, this was Trip's family cabin, and, since I'd never been invited there, it could be a lakeside mansion, for all I knew. The Kipling family has *beaucoup* bucks.

Sheena continued. "The first few days, every time he barked, I jumped, grabbed my gun, and hit the floor. I was sure he was barking because one of those a-holes from The City had tracked me down." She shook her head. "But then I realized the stupid mutt is an indiscriminate barker. He yaps at squirrels, chipmunks, birds. He barked at the leaves. Every time the wind blew, he yelped. Raindrops hitting the cabin? He barked until the rain stopped. And he absolutely howled when there was thunder. All that barking, I about lost my friggin' mind. I had to get out of there, get him back here so we could both relax."

"Okay, but what are you doing *here?* At the convent?"

"I swung by the office, and Germany told me about this case, and I thought maybe I could help. I figured if you were undercover, I could be too. I had Trip drop me off here."

"Does the chief know you're doing this?"

"I figured I'd come here, find you or the chief, and you could fill me in."

"No way, Sheena. This is a delicate thing, here, and the sisters aren't ready for two of us to be snooping around. I've got this case handled. And by the way, where did you get that outfit?"

"From the costume shop. It's a little big, but it's the only one they had."

"Well, nobody here is going to believe you're for real. These sisters don't dress like that."

She eyed my outfit. "They dress like you? What do you call that style—early frump?"

I felt anger rising. "Do not insult these women! They are doing wonderful work in this world—God-given work—and they don't worry about material things."

I was becoming quite a fan of the religious sisters. I even had thoughts about how I might incorporate some of their principles into my life. Not so much that vow of poverty thing, and certainly not that whole celibacy deal—not that I wasn't already living that. But having more time for quiet contemplation appealed to me. I was even open to doing a little more praying, much to my surprise.

Sheena leaned back toward the passenger side window and held up a hand. "Okay, okay, calm down. Nothing personal. So, can I help or not?"

I shook my head. "Nah, I've got this covered, like I said, so you can just go find something else to work on. I've heard about some vandalism and break-ins around town, and some businesses are asking for extra security around Halloween. Maybe the chief can hook you up with something."

"Vandalism? Security? Big deal! I should have stayed in The City where they have *real* crime."

"Well, maybe there *isn't* enough crime to suit you here in 'the sticks.'" I air-quoted. "Maybe you *should* go back where you came from!" I'd had enough of her attitude toward Three Rivers.

"Maybe I will!"

Oh, joy! She'll leave TriMak, and I'll have her-office-that-is-really-mine.

She went on with a sneer. "And I'll take Germany back to The City with me, and then you can go back to your little front desk and running the show."

Back to running things again as office manager, now that I was finally, officially an investigator? No thanks.

She added, with an extra sneer. "And then you'll have Trip all to yourself!"

I fumed. "That again? Are you f—" I caught myself. "Are you flippin' kidding me? You are one-hundred-and-ten-percent dead wrong about that! Trip and I are *not*—nor have we *ever* been—involved with each other, other than in a strictly business sense! From what I can see, he is completely crazy about you, Sheena. And as far as I'm concerned, you're welcome to him!"

She stared out the side window and then turned to me, letting out a long breath. "Okay, Prentice, I get it. You're on this case. You've got it covered. You don't need me."

Was she getting teary-eyed? I dismissed the notion. Sheena was too tough for that.

Eyes wide, she said, "But grant me this. If you *do* need help, will you call me? Seriously, I mean it." She grabbed my arm. "Please, please, please? Promise? Day or night, call me, okay?"

I stared at her hand until she pulled it back. "Fine, Sheena. I don't need help, but if I do, I'll call you."

"Promise?"

"Yes. Absolutely."

Like I've said before, sometimes you say things like, "Yes, absolutely yes," when you really mean, "No, no way, absolutely not."

As she opened the passenger door, I remembered the strange car. "Wait, Sheena. Earlier this week, Germany and I saw a car outside TriMak. Out-of-state plates."

She paled, and her eyes went wide. "What kind of car?"

"A yellow Camaro. Glass-packs. Loud."

She started to shake. "Holy shit. He found me. Son of a—"

"Who found you?"

She shook her head. "No, no, no."

I grabbed her sleeve. "Sheena! Who? Who found you?"

She looked at me, terror in her eyes. "My ex, that's who. I cannot believe he found me here." She called Trip on her cell and asked him to pick her up, then took off down the alley to meet him, hollering loud enough for the neighborhood to hear, "Shit! Holy, holy shit!"

I cringed. Such language from a nun.

CHAPTER THIRTY-NINE

THE FRIGHT NIGHT CARNIVAL is the biggest annual fundraiser for Holy Assumption. With the whole town in the Halloween mood, the carnival draws a huge crowd. Parents, children, and school staff and students are all in costume. Tiny pillowcase ghosts, witches, clowns, celebrity masks.

One family dressed as the characters from Toy Story—Buzz Lightyear dad, Jessie the Cowgirl mom, little cowboy Woody, and baby Potato Head. Adorable.

Little doctors and nurses, Red Riding Hood and the Big Bad Wolf. Cruella de Vil with a stuffed toy dalmatian. Assorted rabbits, kittens, dogs, and one little boy, the mini-me version of the student dressed as Abe Lincoln.

The students and some parent volunteers manned the carnival games. Ring toss, Nerf darts, a fishing game with magnets on the end of the line, kids trying to snag cardboard fish with paperclips on their noses. A bowling game with little orange bowling balls with jack-o-lantern faces rolled between a lane formed by hay bales, to hit little wooden scarecrows. A table for "spider races" where kids blew through straws to propel black plastic spiders to the finish line.

Hay bales and cornstalks lined the walls of the gym, festooned with garlands of fake autumn leaves, alongside pumpkins and ears of dried corn. Three Holy Assumption students sat at a long table, decorating pumpkins with colored markers. Quite artistic. Garrett Nance was one of them, smiling as he applied a steady hand to a pumpkin face.

A row of decorated pumpkins was lined up at the end of the table, free to take with a freewill donation. A plastic pumpkin bucket was filling quickly with money.

Sister Petronilla had told me that sisters were free to add "a little something" to their attire, "keeping it conservative, of course." She gave a tug on the red and white polka-dot scarf she'd tied around her neck. Sister Bernadette wore an official nurse's hat—probably her own from back in the day.

I didn't have anything to add to Mary Agnes's outfit, but that was okay because her outfit *was* my costume. Nobody knew that, of course.

We walked around, admiring others' creativity and laughing with students and family members. I spotted the chief standing near the doorway and left Petronilla talking with Buzz Lightyear and Cowgirl Jessie.

Chief Bronson had obviously decided his Father Percival costume would be good enough for the evening. I greeted him and commented on the good job the students had done with the decorations.

He chuckled. "They still have some of the same stuff we had back in the day, like that scarecrow. I recognize those overalls."

He pointed to the stuffed figure set on a hay bale by the

gym door. It wore faded denim overalls with a John Deere logo, a ragged plaid shirt, and old running shoes. The stuffed hands wore gardening gloves. A garden pitchfork lay across its lap, and bits of straw stuck out here and there from the wrists and the neck. A floppy straw hat sat above the big eyes and happy smile painted on its stuffed, burlap sack head.

Pretty standard scarecrow in my estimation. Nowhere near as creepy as Germany's creation back at TriMak. "You sure it's the same one, Ch—uh, Father? Not likely it would survive fifty years of Halloweens."

We got closer. The chief leaned in to examine it. "I suppose not." At that moment, the scarecrow grabbed the chief's arm.

Father Percival jumped back. "Holy Moth—" He caught himself and looked at me. "Forgive me, Sister."

I bowed my head and said, "No worries, Father." I turned to the scarecrow. "What a great costume. You can't even tell there's a person inside."

The chief, recovering from the shock, agreed. "Yeah. Great costume. But it should come with a warning label."

The scarecrow was chuckling as we left.

The chief and I wandered around the carnival as he told me he'd talked with Doctor G. Finlay at the hospital. "Nothing out of the ordinary with Sister Mary Agnes's death. Accidental fall. Case closed."

In my experience as an investigator, people just see the obvious. They believe what they see and don't ask questions. But my job is to question everything, ask the 'what if" questions and dig until I find the truth. The real truth, not just what seems to be.

Sister Celeste announced that the silent auction would be ending in five minutes. "Anyone who still wishes to bid on our lovely prize should do so now." Several people headed out of the gym.

A little while later, the chief and I were at the door by the scarecrow when I spotted Archie.

I elbowed the chief and pointed. "What's Archie doing here?"

"Free country," he said. "He'd win a prize for that costume."

"Shame on you, Erwin," I said, imitating Sister Celeste.

He scowled at me. "I'm going to follow him and question him myself. See if I can figure out what he meant by that 'Gordon' business."

I felt a little miffed that the chief thought he could get more information out of Archie than "Gordon" and references to outer space. But whatever.

I told the chief I wanted to talk with Perry Cuthbert about the painting. I went to the classroom across from the gym. The silent auction winner had been announced, and the painting, "Ellie's Dance," had been wrapped and carried off. Perry Cuthbert was chatting with Sister Doris, as she tidied the classroom. I approached, and she introduced me.

"Sister Doris, I wonder if I might have a moment alone with Mr. Cuthbert?"

She nodded and left the room.

"Call me Perry, please, Sister," he said.

"Perry, could you tell me more about your beautiful painting? Why call it "Ellie's Dance"?"

He paused and took a breath. "A student I knew."

"Ellie Randolph?"

"Yes."

"She died, I heard. Were you close?"

He wiped a tear away. "Yes, we were. Very close."

I decided to tell him the truth. I closed the classroom door. "Mr. Cuthbert—Perry—I'm not really a sister here. I'm a private investigator—Mackenzie Prentice is my real name. I'm trying to ascertain if Sister Mary Agnes's death was accidental. From what I've learned so far, there is some secret something that happened long ago that Mary Agnes felt guilty about. Someone sent her threatening notes, warning her to keep silent. I have a hunch it had something to do with Ellie Randolph. Do you have any idea what that might have been?"

He heaved a sigh and sat in one of the classroom chairs. "Have a seat, Ms. Prentice. It's a long story, and I've held on to it long enough."

Perry Cuthbert was a young art teacher back when Ellie Randolph was an art history major, as Lillian Sharp had said. "I know it was wrong, but she was such a lovely young thing, and I was, well, in my thirties and unattached. We hit it off and started dating on the sly. I would have lost my position if anyone had found out. I didn't want to end things, but she was afraid her parents would find out. We'd sneak off to her father's hotel, and she said it was only a matter of time before one of the staff there told him what was going on. We broke it off. And a couple weeks later, she was gone."

He looked at the ceiling. "She's been my guardian angel all these years. It's why I created the painting years ago, and now I'm ready to let it go."

It was obvious he knew nothing about Ellie's abortion, and I didn't feel I should tell him. *Let Ellie's secret stay buried with her.*

Twenty minutes later, Perry Cuthbert headed back to the city airport and then on to New York. He'd told me his story. Now I had to figure out how it all fit with Sister Agnes's death.

I went back to the gym, where the last of the families and children were lingering as students and teachers began shutting down the carnival. Sister Celeste Marie was giving orders left and right. "Sister Bernadette, please see that the kitchen area is secure. And will you check the haunted tunnel, please, Sister Michelle?"

I thought, *Aye, aye, Cap'n.,* but I said, "Yes, Reverend Mother." Obedient all the way.

Yards of cobweb material and tissue paper ghosts hung from the tunnel ceiling. A fan humming from somewhere made it all move. The regular light bulbs in the ceiling had been replaced with black lights, giving the white paper ghosts a greenish glow. A recording of creepy music, full of groans and moans filled the air. I walked down the tunnel and came to an extension cord with a power strip attached. I pulled one of the plugs, and the music stopped. Pulling the second plug stopped the fan. The tunnel was silent. I stood, bathed in the glow of the black light for a moment.

The scarecrow came at me from out of nowhere.

CHAPTER FORTY

"WALK!" I RECOGNIZED MRS. Jensen's voice before I turned around. She'd taken off the burlap face. Her long gray hair, usually in a tight bun on top of her head, trailed down her back, bits of straw stuck in it. She held the four-tined garden pitchfork that had been across the lap of her John Deere overalls, as she sat outside the gym. "Down the tunnel! Do what I say, or I'll bury this in your guts!"

I turned and felt the pitchfork in my back. "Where are we going?"

"Just walk!" she barked. She poked me harder.

I had to get away from her. I could try to run back to the gym, but there might still be children between here and there. An angry scarecrow with a pitchfork chasing a nun would give the kids nightmares for years. The only place ahead was the tunnel to the old rectory. I pictured myself running to it, scrambling up the cistern ladder, and out through the hatch above. If—and it was a big if—I could get that hatch open.

I took off running. The sawhorse barricade had been moved

to the midpoint of the tunnel. I ignored the skull and cross-bones warning, DANGER! DO NOT ENTER.

I ran around the barricade, trying to imagine how this was going to play out. Beyond the barricade, the light grew dimmer. I heard her coming, her shoes squeaking on the concrete.

As I ran, I took out my cell phone and texted the chief.

HELP

Did I have a cell signal underground like this? I tried to put the phone back in my sweater pocket, but I missed. The phone clattered to the tunnel floor. No time to stop and pick it up.

A second later, I heard the phone shatter as Mrs. Jensen stomped the life out of it.

Had the text been sent? Would the chief be able to track my location? No time to think about all that. She was hot on my trail.

Her heavy footsteps pounded after me, echoing off the concrete walls. Faster I ran. She slowed, maybe winded. Or maybe she figured I had no escape from here and she could take her sweet time.

I reached the old boards that blocked access to the cistern. The nasty water had a kind of rotten egg smell. I felt the boards in the dim light, feeling for the one that I'd seen earlier hanging by one nail. I wrenched it loose. I held the board high as I turned to defend myself. If I could knock her out, I could get away.

In the dimness, she loomed large, the white of the straw in her hair and the light parts of the plaid shirt glowing eerily in the black light of the tunnel. She came closer. Her breath ragged, she said, "No escape, Sister." She gave a sinister laugh. "I know you've been snooping around. Your skinned knees, your messed clothing. Then I saw you out on the street the other night. On a cell phone. And I heard you and Father talking back by the gym. What's he want with Archie anyway?"

"Just some information. What do you want with me?"

"Your silence. I got Sister Mary Agnes's silence, and now I'll have yours!"

"Whatever you plan to do, you won't get away with it! I'm not really a nun. I'm a cop!" *Lie!* "And Father Percival? He's a cop too. We know all about what you did." *Bluff!* "And the police are on the way right now to arrest you." *Double bluff!* "It's over. You won't get away with this, whatever it is you're planning. You might as well surrender. Put the pitchfork down, Mrs. Jensen. It's over." I tried to sound like I believed that.

Her shrill laugh echoed through the tunnel. "No, if I'm going out, you're going with me."

Out? She didn't mean going out of the tunnel, I knew that.

She lunged at me with the pitchfork.

I dodged. *Keep her talking. They like to confess at times like this.* I'd learned that from previous cases. Perps love to brag to me before they try to kill me. "Why did you do it?" I yelled.

She scoffed. "I heard Sister Mary Agnes praying, heard her mumbling and muttering about sin and death. Saying she had to confess. I couldn't let her do that. She was going to tell everyone."

"Tell everyone what?"

"That Hannah isn't really mine."

"So, you adopted a daughter. Big deal!"

She gave a derisive snort. "We didn't *adopt* her! She survived the abortion, and Sister Mary Agnes just gave her to us."

I thought a moment. Abortion. I'd seen it in the little notebook. "PG" and "D&C" on several entries. Which one was this?

Mrs. Jensen poked the pitchfork toward me. I bent at the waist to dodge the tines.

She yelled, "Don't you get it? Sister Mary Agnes was going to tell the police, and they'd take my Hannah away. Those rich Randolphs already have everything. And we'd be left with nothing. Nothing!"

Chunks of the puzzle fell into place. *Keep her talking.* "Ellie Randolph was Hannah's mother."

Mrs. Jensen poked again. I dodged again. She hissed, "Yes, yes, yes, but what kind of mother was she going to be? She didn't even want the baby!"

Another jab. Another dodge. She went on. "I couldn't have children. I was like Hannah in the Bible. I prayed for a baby for years. When Sister Mary Agnes gave her to us, it was a sign from God. A miracle. That's why we named her Hannah. And we've kept the secret all these years. We made up a story that it was my sister's baby. That she'd died in childbirth, and her husband had died so nobody else could take the baby."

I said, "So Ellie Randolph had the abortion but didn't know the baby survived." Another fact.

"She didn't want to know. She didn't want her own baby. The slut!"

"And then Ellie died."

With a sneer, Mrs. Jensen said, "Well, she had a little help. Just to be sure she didn't change her mind."

I felt a chill as my stomach went into a knot. "Help? What do you mean?"

"Oh, a little something in her bedtime tea," she said with

pride. "A little something I make from lily of the valley. I have so much in my garden."

"My grandmother has lily of the valley in her garden as well. It's beautiful." *Keep her talking. Stall for time.*

She looked at the ceiling. "Beautiful, yes, and poisonous. Bet you didn't know that. It's the May flower. It represents sweetness and purity."

Oh, the irony.

"I've had it in my garden since before Hannah was born. She was born on the fifteenth of May."

Hannah was born one week before her birth mother died, not even knowing her daughter existed. How sad.

I needed to keep Mrs. Jensen talking, hoping the chief got my message and that help was on the way. "I had no idea lily of the valley was poisonous."

She smiled. "My yes, it is. Most people don't know that. I make a very special concoction that goes in the bedtime tea. If you were a tea drinker, you could have sampled it yourself."

I shuddered at the thought. *Thank God Gram got me hooked on coffee at an early age.* "You put it in Ellie Randolph's tea? And in Sister Mary Agnes's tea? Weren't you concerned the medical examiner would find it after they died?"

"No. Ellie Randolph officially died from an overdose of pain pills. And Sister's death was a fall. Nobody checked for anything else. And I can't depend on Mother Angeline forgetting it all. She's kept silent so far, but she might have a good moment and ruin everything."

"Mother Angeline was there?" *Keep her talking.*

"Yes, she was an army nurse in the Second World War, before she became a nun. She assisted Doctor Phelps with the girls."

Army nurse, nun, protector of the community. Keeper of secrets.

Mrs. Jensen shouted suddenly. "Enough talking!" She adjusted her grip on the pitchfork. I readied myself for another lunge. I gripped the wooden board harder.

"One more thing," I said. *Sister Michelle Columbo channeling her TV hero.* "Tell me how you got Sister into the bell tower. That was very clever."

She told me how she lured Sister Mary Agnes there, and when Mary Agnes wouldn't promise to keep silent, she pushed her down the stairs.

I took a shot. "You tracked mud into the tower when you lured her up there." *Garden. Mud.* "That proves you were there." Another chunk of the puzzle. "Archie tried to tell us. He said Gordon, but he meant garden."

She said, "He calls me Mrs. Garden. I give him vegetables when he stops by."

"Forensics will match that mud to your shoes."

She got quiet for a moment, probably considering that idea. "Ha! I'll burn those shoes after I kill you."

Keep her talking. "You've kept the secret, but your daughter Hannah never had a chance to know her real family."

"Her *real* family? We *are* her real family! The only family she's ever known!"

She lunged again. I swung the board hard, and the pitchfork flew from her hands and clanked to the concrete floor of the tunnel. She paused, then gave a warrior yell and lunged at me.

I dropped the board and spun away from her. She grabbed me from behind. She had me around the waist, pressing her fists into my diaphragm as she lifted me off the ground. *Hardest Heimlich ever.* I couldn't breathe.

I thrashed and kicked my feet at her legs. The padding in the John Deere overalls protected her shins. I slammed my head backward as hard as I could. My skull connected with her nose.

She screeched. "Damn you! You broke my nose!"

She dropped me, and I fell forward, both knees of Gram's final pair of pantyhose ripping as I hit the concrete. Anxious had a thought. *Gram's gonna be so pissed!*

Badass had another thought. *Least of our worries. Get up and fight this bitch!*

I crawled forward and grabbed the pitchfork by the tine end, stood, and swung it at her. She grabbed the wooden handle.

The iron tines scraped into my palms. We did a little dance there, as she held one end and I the other. Around and around we went.

Badass reminded me, *First one who lets go loses.*

We danced closer and closer to the cistern. At the edge of the cistern, she swung the pitchfork hard to the left. Like a game of crack the whip, I swung with it. The backs of my knees hit the low wall, and I went backward into the water.

She gave a triumphant laugh and shoved her end of the pitchfork toward me as I fell. In her delight at having bested me, she forgot to let go. As I fell into the nasty water, she came right along with me, pitchfork and all.

The shock of the cold water stunned me. I let the tines go as I gasped air in and went under, holding my breath. My bottom met the bottom of the cistern. I sort of bounced up to standing. The water was almost hip-deep.

In the semi-darkness, I could make out her shape. We faced off.

She still had the pitchfork. I had nothing but my wits. Snarky snarked, *So, you're unarmed.*

She poked the tines at me, and I grabbed hold of the metal. I pushed back. She yanked the handle, and the tines slipped from my fingers. I felt warm blood ooze into my palms.

You can't really run in hip-deep water. This fight was pretty much slo-mo.

Suddenly, she dropped the pitchfork, crouched, and then propelled herself out of the water.

The full weight of her, soggy stuffing and all, knocked me backward. She pressed me under the water, her knees against my right side.

I took in a mouthful of swamp, then held my breath as long as I could. My lungs started to burn as I thrashed against her.

My survival instinct kicked in. With a rush of adrenaline I twisted to my left, pressed my hands against the bottom of the cistern, and pushed upward with all my might. She rolled off me, splashing backward and cursing.

I scrambled to my feet, gasping for air. I moved toward where I thought she'd dropped the pitchfork. My foot hit it, I reached under the water and brought it up. I turned, aiming the tines toward her as she rose up out of the water, like an angry sea monster.

Both of us gasping for air, I managed to shout, "Enough! Stop right there."

She bent over from the waist, breathing heavily. A standoff. She had the weight, plus the added weight of her scarecrow stuffing.

But I had the advantage of youth. And now, of course, the pitchfork.

What now, Sherlock? How you gonna get out of this cistern? I thought of that old brain teaser with the fox and the two geese trying to cross a river. *Or were they ducks?*

If I tried to climb out, she'd pull me back.

If I let her climb out first, she'd get away.

Badass had a thought. *Knock her out and drag her to the cops.* Rational Me took charge. "Back away. Stand over there."

"Fine," she said as she stepped toward the opposite side of the cistern. "I'm too tired to fight anymore."

I knew she was lying, that she was just regrouping before she tried to kill me again. But since I had the pitchfork firmly in my hands, it was Advantage: Sister Michelle Columbo.

I stood there shivering in the cold, scummy water, clothes soaked, pantyhose shredded, palms bleeding. I had a moment lamenting the likely demise of my best black leather shoes, one of which was somewhere at the bottom of this cistern. The other was soggy on my right foot as I held this murderer at bay. I braced myself for her next move. How was I going to get out of this?

Without warning, she dove under the slime, and in a second, I felt her hands around my ankles, pulling at me, trying to knock me over. I drove the pitchfork down into the water and felt the contact with her body.

She thrashed in the water, then came up screaming. "You stabbed me! On purpose! My arm is bleeding!"

I couldn't see well enough to assess the truth of that, but wished, at that moment, for sharks in the water.

"Back away!" I screamed at her, then repeated her threat as I poked her stomach with the pitchfork. "Don't make *me* bury this in *your* guts."

She stepped backward and bumped into the ladder at the side of the cistern.

I shouted an order. "Turn around and wrap your arms around the ladder."

She started to protest.

I yelled, "Shut up! Hug it! Now!"

She heaved a sigh and obeyed.

I tore off Gram's soggy pantyhose and used them to tie her—admittedly a little more tightly than absolutely necessary—to the ladder.

A second later, I heard the most beautiful sound in all of creation—the chief shouting, "Mack? Where are you?"

The cavalry had arrived.

CHAPTER FORTY-ONE

FATHER PERCIVAL AND SISTER Sheena, still in that ridiculous nun costume, stood above the cistern. Police-grade flashlights in hand, they trained their beams on the two of us in the water. Germany held a third flashlight.

Sheena had her gun in her right hand, trained on Mrs. Jensen. "Make a move. I dare you," she said.

Badass was impressed. *Go ahead. Make my day.*

Mrs. Jensen started to accuse me of pushing her into the cistern, trying to drown her. She whined about me stabbing her with the pitchfork, unprovoked. *As if!*

Sheena glared. "Shut up, or I'll shoot you."

Mrs. Jensen went mute.

I waded over to the edge of the cistern. Germany and the chief pulled me up out of the stinky water. Germany wrinkled his nose. "Whew! Nasty!"

I started to shiver. He took off his TriMak windbreaker and wrapped it around my shoulders. "Thanks, Foghorn."

"Anytime, Wonder Chick," he said.

I noticed Trip standing behind the chief, holding a tennis racket. He gave me a sheepish look. "All I could find," he said with a shrug.

Mrs. Jensen screeched from the cistern. "What about me? Get me out of here! I'm an old lady. I can't climb out of here by myself!"

The chief said, "Reinforcements are on the way. They'll take care of you." We left her screaming and swearing as we headed back through the tunnel. We met Heather Sullivan, Officer Dutton, two others in uniform, and two paramedics. The chief explained to Heather who was who and what was what.

Heather gave him a salute and a "Thanks, Chief" as she led the team toward the cistern.

Twenty minutes later, I stood on the church lawn, wrapped in a blanket and smelling like swamp water. Sister Petronilla had brought me a pair of sweatpants, dry socks and slippers.

I suggested to the chief that he tell Heather to get a search warrant to find Mrs. Jensen's muddy shoes. Odds were slim that they'd be useful in the case, but you never know. And also checking Mother Angeline's teacup for traces of lily of the valley. And maybe there'd be evidence of other things in the Jensen's home.

"Maybe Archie will be coherent enough to give a statement too. You never know," I said.

He repeated, "Right, Chickie. You never know," but he looked doubtful.

We watched as Officer Dutton led Mrs. Jensen toward the squad car. I felt the tiniest surge of satisfaction seeing the bandage the paramedics had put on her arm, right where I'd pitchforked her. And I ignored the little twinge of guilt that followed.

Sister Celeste Marie lamented the fact that the police had been called. "We like to handle things within the community," she'd said.

The chief told her, "I understand, but this is a criminal case. No more options for keeping it quiet. Agreed?"

Sister Celeste Marie considered and then nodded. "The time for secrets is over. I defer to your judgment, Erwin."

I stifled a smirk. I was never going to get used to that name.

As Officer Dutton and Mrs. Jensen reached the squad car, Hannah cried, "Mama, no!" She rushed forward.

Mrs. Jensen bent toward her daughter. "Oh, baby. Don't cry, baby. It's okay. Daddy will take care of you."

Mr. Jensen took Hannah to his side, holding her close as Officer Dutton put a palm on Mrs. Jensen's head, guiding her into the back of the squad. Just like on TV.

The chief asked, "What happened in there, Mack?"

I told him and Sister Celeste what I knew.

The chief asked, "What do you know about all this, Sister Celeste?"

She hung her head. "When Miss Prentice told me about the notes, I realized what had happened. Mary Agnes came to me before she died, wanting to tell the truth about what she'd done all those years ago." She took a breath and met the chief's eyes. "I told her to keep quiet. God forgive me."

Mrs. Jensen looked back at her husband and daughter. Unlike other perps you see being arrested, she looked radiant, with a peaceful smile.

Sister Celeste said, "That poor woman."

The chief shot her a look. "Um, that 'poor woman' may have been planning to silence *you* next."

Sister Celeste gave a little shudder and said, "Merciful heaven! I had no idea she was so troubled."

I said, "She masked it well. I wonder how the Randolphs will handle this. And Perry Cuthbert, finding out after over fifty years that he has a daughter."

Sister Celeste shook her head. "No telling what their reaction might be. Shame on all of us. Lord, help us."

I thought how different life could have been for Hannah Jensen, living in luxury as a Randolph and as the daughter of a famous artist. Would she have been happier?

Sister Petronilla walked to me, elbowed me in the side, and then air-quoted. "So, 'Sister Michelle,' you're really a detective?"

I nodded and waited, expecting hurt feelings, disappointment, or maybe anger from her. She surprised me.

"That is so cool! We'll have to do lunch sometime, or dinner. I'd love to know more about your life!"

Petronilla and I were going to be friends. *Cool!*

She asked me, "What do you think will happen to her? To Mrs. Jensen."

I straightened up a little taller and went into professional mode. "No statute of limitations on murder. She confessed to killing Sister Mary Agnes and to putting something in Ellie Randolph's tea. Of course, she might decide to deny all that."

Sister Celeste said, "I might be able to persuade her to accept responsibility. She is a woman of faith, after all."

The chief said, "She'd have to confess since we don't have concrete proof. She'll end up in prison, or an attorney might be able to prove some sort of mental incapacity, and she'd spend the rest of her life in an institution."

Sister Petronilla said, "Her husband and daughter will visit regularly, I'm sure."

"Of course," Sister Celeste said. "We all will, as our Lord Jesus instructed. 'I was in prison, and you visited me.'"

Inspiring, that generosity of spirit. So much of what I'd witnessed in the past week was inspiring. Devotion to duty, consistency in service to others, dedication to prayer. My time with the good sisters of Holy Assumption had touched me, changed me in ways I never expected.

The squad car rolled away, and Doc Jensen walked to us, crumpling his hat in his hands. "I'm mighty sorry, Sisters, and you too, Father, for all the trouble my wife caused here. If I'd known what she was thinking, I could have stopped her."

The chief shook his hand and re-introduced himself—his real self.

Doc grinned. "I knew it! I never forget a face!"

"I have a question for you, Mr. Jensen," I said. "Who cleaned out the medical room in the tunnel?"

"I'd had that on my list for a long time. Somebody'd cleared most of it when I finally got to it, but there were still the big pieces. Since we're fixin' to seal off that tunnel, I wanted to get that stuff out of there and see if I could sell it, make a little money for the convent. When you got stuck in there, I figured I'd better get it done."

Mrs. Jensen must have cleared out the incriminating jars before her husband got to them. What was the protocol for those tiny bodies? *Lost souls.* I heard Mother Angeline's hymn in my head, something about "banished children." *Mother of Mercy.*

Mr. Jensen turned to Sister Celeste. "I'm just so sorry about Sister Mary Agnes. She was good people. It was a miracle when she brought Hannah to us. My wife said it was God's will for us to keep her. I believed her. I hope you can forgive us."

Sister Celeste stepped to him and put a hand on his arm. "Doc, God is the only judge. I'll be praying for you. All of us will be praying for you."

He swiped at a tear with the back of his hand and thanked her. He walked to his daughter, put an arm around her shoulders and guided her toward their house.

What would become of them, I wondered. Would Mr. Jensen lose a wife and a daughter in one fateful night?

Hannah was rightfully a Randolph, and she was also Perry Cuthbert's daughter. She deserved all that entailed. The truth would have to come out, but would that be the best thing for her? I felt sad for her.

I said, "What harm is there in letting Hannah go on with the only family she's ever known?"

The chief shot me a look that said I was being too soft. "Well, her mother is a murderer, for one."

"True, but she was just protecting her family." *Don't be such a sap,* Snarky hissed.

He shook his head at me. "She'd have killed you in that cistern, Chickie, without a second thought."

I shuddered as the certainty of that sank in. I flashed back to the pitchfork. Murderous intent, no question. She'd killed before. Ellie Randolph had overdosed on pain meds, but lily of the valley in her tea contributed to her death. And Sister Mary Agnes, unsteady, confused by the "extra" Mrs. Jensen had been adding to her Sleepy Time Extra bedtime tea, became an easy target on those bell tower stairs. And I had no doubt she'd have killed Mother Angeline, if she thought the old woman could remember what happened.

And she certainly wanted to kill me too. No question.

The night air felt suddenly colder. I hugged the blanket closer as the chief put an arm around my shoulders. "You want to give everyone the benefit of the doubt. But, Chickie, this Mrs. Jensen definitely has a screw loose."

More than one, Snarky agreed.

Out of the corner of my eye, I saw movement in the upstairs window of the convent. I looked up. Mother Angeline stood in her window, in her white nightgown, her long white hair falling to her shoulders. Angelic. And ghostly. She raised a hand, crossed herself, then put her hands together as in prayer. She looked directly at me—at least it felt that way—gave a nod and then smiled.

I smiled back with a little wave. She moved away from the window, the curtains closed, and her light went out.

CHAPTER FORTY-TWO

All Saints' Day, November 1

SATURDAY MORNING, I WAS on the couch in the carriage house, recovering. Trip had sent a huge flower arrangement with a note that said, "Congrats on a job well done!" A nice gesture, but the flowers rankled me just a little. *Do all detectives get flowers after they finish a case? Did Mike Hammer get flowers? Or Sherlock? Or Hercule Poirot? Or Columbo?*

Snarky snarked, *Keep your stupid flowers. Give us our office!*

The chief called my cell to be sure I was okay. He told me Sheena had headed back to Trip's cabin—with Larry, Moe, and Curly for protection from this mysterious ex who'd tracked her down. I can just imagine how thrilled she was about being cooped up with all three dogs.

He also told me that he'd told Sister Celeste about Lucy trying to blackmail her teacher—well, her pretend fake-sister-nun teacher. And the Mother Superior assured him the matter would be "taken care of." Whatever that meant. The kid was desperate, worrying about her grades. Had she gone too far? Absolutely, but I'd been a kid once too, so I hoped the punishment wouldn't be too extreme.

Speaking of kids being desperate not to disappoint their parents, I thought about Ellie Randolph. Her whole situation was just sad. The Randolphs' perfect daughter got knocked up and had an abortion. So afraid of disappointing her parents that she kept all that a secret. So very sad.

Gram tapped on the door and came in with a plate of scrambled eggs and four slices of bacon—extra crispy, just the way I like it. *Mmm, bacon. Way better than flowers.* All parts of me agreed with that. She'd toasted two thick slabs of her homemade white bread and topped it with butter and her home-canned strawberry jam. My kind of soul food.

I told Gram that the weather app said snow might be on the way.

She walked to the door, opened it, and stuck her head out and took a deep breath. "Yep. Smells like snow." She shut the door and sat on the end of the couch. "We never needed any computer back on the farm to tell us what the weather was going to be. My dad's joints ached ahead of the rain. The cows headed to the barn or huddled under the trees. When that happened, we knew bad weather was on the way."

"And your nose can smell the snow," I said with a smile.

She tapped her nose. "Yep. Old reliable! By the way, I spoke with that nice young man who works for you. I told him we're ready whenever he's ready to move in. Now I want to hear all about this 'job well done,' that earned you those beautiful flowers."

I filled her in on what I'd concluded from talking with Heather after she interviewed Mrs. Jensen, and my own chats with Sister Celeste and Perry Cuthbert. The chief had told me what he'd learned from Mother Angeline, who was far more lucid now that she was no longer drinking tea with poison in it.

"Here's what I've put together. Ellie Randolph was secretly seeing Perry Cuthbert. She got pregnant but didn't realize it."

Gram nodded. "That's how it used to be. Girls were so ignorant about such things. Of course, growing up on the farm, we knew everything."

"Feeling off, she went to this Dr. Phelps, in the basement of the dorm. Freaked out when he told her she was pregnant and fairly far along. She didn't want to know anything about the baby, just wanted it to be gone."

Gram said, "Oh, dear. That's just so sad, isn't it? Life is precious, regardless of how it comes into this world."

"Afterward, Ellie was packed off to her room with pain pills. She never knew that the baby—a girl—survived. Tiny, but otherwise healthy. Sister Angeline gave the baby to Sister Mary Agnes, who was just eighteen years old. Told her to take the baby to the Jensens and swear them to secrecy. Said something about it being God's will that they should have the baby, since they'd prayed for so long."

Gram huffed. "Well, just because you prayed doesn't mean you deserve to have something that's not yours!"

"You're right, Gram, but Sister Mary Agnes delivered the baby to the Jensens, and—"

Gram held up a hand. "Wait. How did they explain this to the neighbors?"

"I'm getting there. Hold your horses. They made up some story about Mrs. Jensen's widowed sister dying in childbirth and no other relatives to take the child. I guess nobody ever questioned it."

Gram said, "Oh my. The secrets people carry. You just never know, do you?"

"Sister Mary Agnes, with her declining health, felt the need to confess and be forgiven. She told Sister Celeste she was going to confess all, not just to the priest, but also to the police. Sister Celeste encouraged her to pray some more. Mrs. Jensen overheard that conversation and started following Mary Agnes, hearing her praying and muttering about telling the truth. She even went into the nun's room while she was teaching and read her journal. Probably saw the confession letter in there."

"How rude, reading someone's personal diary!"

"Yeah, Gram. Almost as rude as killing them." I admit that was a tad sarcastic. *Shame on me.*

"Don't be such a smarty pants! Get on with the story!"

"Mrs. Jensen started leaving the notes. Silence. Silence. Silence. She finally decided to put an end to it and pushed Mary Agnes to her death in the bell tower. Everyone—the police included—figured it was an accident. That would have been the end of it all, if Sister Celeste hadn't had 'that feeling' and brought us in."

"Well, thank the good Lord she did!"

"Mrs. Jensen must have realized pretty quickly that I wasn't who I claimed to be. No self-respecting sister comes home with scraped knees like I did." I looked at Gram. "Sorry I ruined all your pantyhose, by the way."

She waved a hand. "Never mind about that. Get back to the story!"

"Mrs. Jensen started watching me more closely. She over-heard me talking with the chief, saw us leaving in his car. When I was trying to get information from Archie—she knew he'd been in the bell tower—she was afraid it was only a matter of time before I made the connection. I thought Archie was saying 'Gordon,' but he was trying to say 'Garden." He called her Mrs. Garden."

"How did you end up locked in that basement room?"

"Oh yeah. Mrs. Jensen was going in there to destroy any evidence of what happened back in the 1960s. She heard me coming, so she hid in another part of the tunnel. Then she locked me in while she figured out what to do with me. Meanwhile, her husband heard me shouting while he was doing his nightly rounds, and he let me out. But Mrs. Jensen figured that I'd found something in that room and needed to be silenced. And long story short, that's how we ended up in the cistern."

"Whew!" Gram said when I finished.

"Even though Mrs. Jensen has been arrested, Gram, you still can't tell Velma, okay? The court outcome could be compromised if there's too much, uh,"—I wanted to say gossip, but I said—"too much publicity."

"Don't worry," Gram said. "I could never even remember all of that to tell Velma. Here now, finish your toast."

Yes, ma'am. I polished off the last bite, and then Gram followed me up to the loft and tucked me in for a nap. Raindrops pelted the double window across from the foot of the bed.

Gram said, "*Kuuntele sadetta*, my father would say."

Gram's Finnish father had lots of sayings. "What's that mean?"

"Listen to the rain," she said as she tucked the blankets tighter around me, before planting a light kiss on my forehead. She went down the stairs, and I heard the door close softly behind her.

Clayton and crew had completed the repairs while I was at the convent. Just in time, too, because the rain had become steady and relentless. Straight down. No wind. Soaking, drenching everything.

I listened to it thrumming on the roof of the carriage house, pelting the remaining leaves on the oaks, the yellow maples long since stripped bare by the wind and rain. I pictured the puddles forming in Gram's yard, filling the depressions under the swing set, where two generations of her grandchildren have played.

Stuart Klump, local TV weather guy, had said to expect the rain to turn to snow later.

Chloe purred at my side as I listened to the waterfall of rain singing a song of renewal. The water of life. The sisters' appreciation for everything in this world had rubbed off on me. The simplicity of their lives, the gratitude they expressed for the smallest of things.

I was grateful to be warm and dry. I dozed off, and when I awoke, the rain had turned to thick glops of snow. I got up and stood at the window, watching it fall. The first of the season, covering the ground like forgiveness. A multitude of sins disappearing under the blanket of pure, unadulterated white. Bits of an old hymn, heard at Our Savior's, floated through my mind.

Sin had left a crimson stain . . . He washed it white as snow.

THAT NIGHT, GRAM FIXED A ROAST with red potatoes, gravy, and her baking powder biscuits, which are always the just-right combination of soft on the inside and chewy on the outside. We were at the table. Greg and Sarah and their three kids, Gram and Nathan, my mom and Duncan.

After dinner, Gram brought out one of her amazing coconut custard pies with mile-high meringue and a pan of brownies with inch-thick chocolate frosting. Since it is impossible to choose just one, I had a little of both.

In the middle of dessert, Duncan cleared his throat. "Family?" We looked at him. He said, "I have something to say." He stood a moment, moved his chair back, and looked at my mother. "Barbara, you have given me nothing but grief. You've run away, you've argued, and you are absolutely the most stubborn woman I've ever known."

Snarky agreed. *He's got that right.*

My mother had tears in her eyes.

Anxious Me felt awful. *No, no, no, Duncan! You can't dump her in front of the whole family.*

Then Duncan reached his hand out and touched the pink spot on my mother's cheek, left over from the meatloaf incident. Something in that touch—ever-so-tender—brought a lump to my throat. I blinked back tears.

Duncan dropped to one knee in front of my mother. She gave a little gasp as she covered her mouth with a hand, wide-eyed. Just like in the movies.

Duncan's deep voice rumbled. "Barbara Marie Prentice, I love you. I promise to be faithful, to be by your side, supporting and encouraging you for the rest of my days." He pulled a ring from his pocket, with a huge rock that sparkled under Gram's dining room chandelier. "Will you be my wife?"

My mother stared at him, blinked back tears, and for a moment, I was afraid *she* was going to dump *him* in front of the whole family.

I held my breath. Then she started laugh-crying as she threw her arms around his neck. "Yes, Duncan, yes. Yes!"

I jumped to my feet, applauding. Greg, Sarah, and their kids followed suit. Gram wiped tears with her napkin. Everybody started hugging everyone else.

Nathan looked up from his dinner. "What's all the fuss?"

Gram explained, and Nathan called to Duncan, "Well done, my boy! Well done!"

A perfect rom-com kind of ending.

I looked on, thinking about Nick. And then thinking about Vince. Lonely Me asked, *Which one would do something like Duncan just did?*

I smiled. What Duncan had just done was a Nick kind of thing.

Yes, Nick. Definitely, Nick.

That is, of course, if he'd still have me.

MY COUSIN KRISSY

A Mackenzie Prentice Mystery

Every family has its secrets. I was sure I knew all of ours. It turns out I was dead wrong.

MACK'S COUSIN KRISTEN, AKA **Krazy Krissy**, has been out of the family picture for a couple of decades. Nobody is quite sure where she's been or what she's been doing. And she's not sharing. Now, just before Thanksgiving, Krissy shows up with a suitcase full of secrets and a dead body in the trunk. She begs Mack to help her unwind the mess she's gotten herself into before it's too late.

Mackenzie Prentice is thirty-five, has a touch of OCD, is addicted to sugar, may occasionally drink too much, and has those voices in her head commenting on her choices. In this sixth book of the Mackenzie Prentice Mysteries, Cousin Krissy's crisis, of course, becomes Mack's problem and leads to life-threatening events. Will Mack be able to save Krissy from her situation? Will Mack live long enough to be her mom's maid of honor? And if she does, there's the bigger question: who will be her plus-one?

Author Mary Pierce shares her home in Wisconsin with her husband, Terry, and their goldendoodle, Sammy, named after their favorite pizza place. You can find Mary on Substack: *Old Woman, New Life by Mary Pierce* at marypierce.substack.com.

ACKNOWLEDGMENTS

THANKS TO YOU FIRST, DEAR READER, for spending some of your precious time in Three Rivers with Mackenzie and the gang. You keep reading, and I'll keep writing.

Thank you, Michelle Rayburn (missionandmedia.com) for cheerleading, editing, designing, and consulting. Your leadership and generosity in this indie publishing paradigm is amazing.

Thank you to Joe Coughlin for generously sharing his expertise in law enforcement. (Errors in that area are strictly my own.)

Thanks to the family clan. Alex, Katy, Liz, Jenny, Laura, Dan, partners, and children. So grateful to have you all.

Thanks to my fellow Substack writers who inspire me with their love of language and vulnerability. I draw inspiration—and courage—from all of you.

And to Aron Croft (hiddenadhd.com) and the PTA family, thank you for your support, coaching (Deb), and for all the study hall pals (Martha, Tammy, Renee, Ruth, Lili, Hannah, Lindsey, Scott, Tim, Peter, Annie, Heidi, and the rest) keeping me focused. Altogether now: "Consistency over intensity! HooYah!"

To faithful early readers: Maureen, Dan, Kelly, Neenee, Janis, Melyssa, Fern, Laura, Paula, Mary Lee, Jane, Nancy, Liz, Jessie, Deirdre, Ashley, Barbara, and Mack's growing base of fans, thank you for your enthusiasm in spreading the word. I love you all!

Finally, thank you to my darling Terry for four decades of love and encouragement. I'd be lost without you.

ACKNOWLEDGMENTS

ABOUT THE AUTHOR

MARY PIERCE IS THE AUTHOR OF the Mackenzie Prentice Mysteries, a lifelong dream. She is also the author of three books of humorous inspiration/memoir published by Harper Collins/Zondervan: *When Did I Stop Being Barbie and Become Mrs. Potato Head*; *Confessions of a Prayer Wimp*; and *When Did My Life Become a Game of Twister*, along with hundreds of articles and a humor column for a national magazine.

Mary spent twenty years as a keynote humorist, bringing laughter and encouragement to audiences at women's wellness events and retreats around the country.

She left the speaking circuit to care for her aging mother, who had dementia. After six years as primary family caregiver, Mary returned to school, earning a master's degree in Clinical Mental Health Counseling at the age of sixty. As a licensed psychotherapist, she works with adults who are dealing with depression, anxiety, and life changes, specializing in trauma reprocessing and support for family caregivers.

Mary enjoys sketching, art journaling, and messing around with collage and assemblage as a mixed media artist. (Paint? Glue? Ripping paper? What's not to love?)

She and her husband, Terry, share six children and eleven grandchildren. They make their home in Wisconsin with their goldendoodle, Sammy.

You can find Mary on Substack: *Old Woman, New Life by Mary Pierce* at www.marypierce.substack.com.